# GYM
# BOYS

# GYM BOYS

## GAY EROTIC STORIES

EDITED BY
SHANE ALLISON

Published in the United States by Cleis Press, an imprint of Start Midnight, LLC, 221 River Street, 9th Floor, Hoboken, NJ 07030.

Printed in the United States.
Cover design: Scott Idleman/Blink
Cover photograph: iStockphoto
Text design: Frank Wiedemann
First Edition.
10 9 8 7 6 5 4 3 2 1

Trade paper ISBN: 978-1-62778-124-4
E-book ISBN: 978-1-62778-179-4

"Bagged," by Jake Rich, previously appeared in Ultimate Gay Erotica 2009, edited by Jesse Grant (Alyson Books).

# Contents

vii    *Introduction*

1    *One More* • JAY STARRE
11    *The Ropes* • GREGORY L. NORRIS
22    *Means to an End* • ROB ROSEN
33    *Helping Rufus* • BOB VICKERY
46    *Heart On* • MICHAEL BRACKEN
57    *Jockstraps* • OLEANDER PLUME
69    *Steel Dreams* • LOGAN ZACHARY
83    *The Artistry of Steam* • BRENT ARCHER
95    *Birthday Workout* • JEFF MANN
112    *Gym Friends* • FOX LEE
126    *Montgomery Gymnos* • SHANE ALLISON
136    *Mr. Sampson's Muscle Palace* • R. W. CLINGER
150    *Pumping Ivan* • LANDON DIXON
159    *Working Out the Kinks* • KATYA HARRIS
171    *Safari* • SASHA PAYNE
185    *Bagged* • JAKE RICH

197    *About the Authors*
200    *About the Editor*

# INTRODUCTION

Oh my god, there he was on the treadmill, shirtless, glistening with sweat that trickled down a muscled torso. I thought of how I had a long way to go before I looked like that: drop-dead gorgeous. I was fed up with being overweight, and got the recommendation from my physician that I should drop a minimum of fifty pounds. I finally grew the balls to join a gym. I grew weary of only walking past the window of Gold's, watching everyone but me change their lives. I didn't just want to shed the pounds for reasons of health, but also so I would no longer seem invisible to the hotties that pranced around the local gay clubs. Damn, this guy was handsome. I knew I wouldn't be able to snag a man like him on my best day.

The first day I laid eyes on him I was about to put off my workout for the umpteenth time when I saw him saunter into the gym. He cut me the cutest smile when he walked past me. This guy was the embodiment of hot. If you looked up *gorgeous* in the dictionary, you would probably find his pretty face. This beauty was all the encouragement I needed to take that chance.

I went in, filled out forms, signed my John Hand job, I mean, Hancock, on the dotted line, paid my sixteen-dollar membership and followed that muscle-lust stud into the workout area of the gym. I was hypnotized by his stunning good looks. Where in the hell had this guy been all my life? Luckily, the treadmill next to him was vacant. To see his muscles flexing under sinewy skin was enough to make my dick hard. I had never been on a treadmill, and started to fumble around with the contraption, not having the slightest idea what I was doing, yet it provided the perfect excuse to ask for this bohunk's assistance. When I asked him for help, he looked annoyed, breathing heavy, dripping with sweat. "Sorry to bother you, but do you know how to operate this?"

He stopped his own machine to step over to assist me. "How fast do you want to go?"

*As fast or as slow as you want, baby,* I thought. "Do you want to walk or run?" I would have preferred to walk, but I didn't want the object of my affection to think that I was a lightweight, so I decided to run it out. I told him that a good jog to get the blood flowing and the heart pumping would be good enough. He instructed me on how to use the buttons and what they were used for, informing me that I could use this and that button to quicken or slow down my speed. When I asked him how often he frequented the gym in some sad attempt to break the ice, I felt like the biggest loser. As soon as that cornball of a question slipped out of my mouth, I wanted to reel it back in.

"About six days a week." He asked me if it was my first time at Gold's.

"Is it that obvious?"

He smiled all pretty. "I've seen you standing outside a few times, looking through the window."

I was so embarrassed. "You must have thought I was some kind of pervert or something."

"Not at all. I was like you once: struggling to take that first step. I'm glad that you made it in."

I switched on the machine and began to jog at a steady pace. It wasn't long before I started to breathe heavy, but I doubt that it had anything to do with any treadmill. I'm the type who likes to see instant results the moment after I'm done working out, wanting the weight to melt off. "I'm Shane by the way," I told him.

"Steve." What a beautiful name for a beautiful man. I wanted to tattoo it on my ass. *Owned and operated by Steve.* "So do you have a goal weight that you would like to meet?"

"I'm trying to lose about fifty pounds."

"That sounds like a good, healthy size for your height. I think you would look amazing." Oh my god, had he just said I would look amazing?

"Thank you, I hope so."

"As long as you keep working hard and being persistent, you shouldn't have a problem meeting your goal." Steve's words of encouragement were exactly what I needed to hear in order to keep going, considering I felt like I was close to fainting from exhaustion. I adjusted the speed to slow things down.

Steve and I spent a good hour and a half working out and talking, then we hit the showers. I wasn't sure how comfortable I would be showering with another man, but I had to see this guy in the buff. His dick looked to be about eight inches while his ass was bubbled and firm. I would have given anything to cop a feel, to wrap my lips around his horse-hung dick. I would glance down at it as I soaped up. I was scared shitless he might have caught me staring, but he never did. My dick hardened to the sight of Steve's well-endowed appendage. I wish I could say that we got up to something, but Steve showered, got out and dried off the ass I wanted to smother my face in, and left. "I guess I will see you around," he said.

Now that I had taken that plunge, I made working out a six-day-a-week regiment, all so I could run into Hot Steve. I not only met my goal weight, but I lost twenty more pounds and was quickly burning fat and gaining muscle. After about four weeks I started to see a difference. No one would ever call me Fat Albert again. I could finally see my dick without having to bend over, thanks partly to Steve. The losing weight part, I mean. He and I not only became friends, but loyal fuck buddies, so all of the fantasies and rock-hard dreams I had about him had finally come true.

The sixteen gym-sational stories I have assembled here will, taunt, tease and titillate thanks to some of my favorite gay erotica veterans like Bob Vickery, Gregory L. Norris, Rob Rosen, Jay Starre, Logan Zachary, Landon Dixon, Jeff Mann, R. W. Clinger and Michael Bracken, as well as the rising stars of gay erotica: Brent Archer, Fox Lee, Katya Harris, Oleander Plume, Sasha Payne and Jake Rich. I hope you enjoy reading these stories over and over as much as I have.

Shane Allison
Tallahassee, Florida

# ONE MORE

## Jay Starre

One More was the name of Raphael's personal training business and when his new young client had asked about it, he explained.

"What use is a trainer if he isn't asking for one more?"

Raphael winked and slapped Tommy lightly on the butt as they made their way into the training area late that Sunday night. The redhead flinched, not expecting the friendly slap. It was hardly unwelcome though. Raphael was a dusky-skinned Brazilian immigrant with raven-black hair and big brown eyes; handsome as hell and with a body to die for. Tommy hired him the moment they met, not only in the hopes of learning more about training but also for the chance to spend some time with the gorgeous trainer.

"One more, I'm up for that," he replied enthusiastically, hardly imagining Raphael's training method would go way beyond what the twenty-two-year-old could possibly have expected. Or hoped for!

On Sunday evenings the Laguna Beach Gym closed early at

9:00 p.m. and they had the place to themselves. Raphael had arranged it with Bradley, the desk attendant who seemed to be his buddy. Tommy appreciated it, considering he was busy on the beach working long hours this time of year as a lifeguard.

Raphael was a smooth talker with impeccable English and was all smiles as he began to put the redhead through his paces. "That's it, Tommy. Lean back on your heels and push upward with your entire lower body, not just your thighs. You want to engage those glutes, don't you?"

The squats had him straining and sweating, which served the purpose of warming him up adequately. He would need to be warmed up for what followed, although he didn't yet know it.

"Now for some pull-ups. I'm going to wrap your wrists and attach the straps to the chin-up bar. That way you can dangle from the bar and stretch your spine after each set. I warn you though; this is going to be brutal. I expect you to go all out. Are you ready for that?"

Tommy nodded vigorously. His cock had risen up hard and twitching the moment Raphael had slapped his ass, and was still tenting his baggy green workout shorts. He was pretty sure the trainer had noticed it, although he had politely made no mention of it.

The short redhead stood on a crate to reach the bar while the taller Brazilian put the wrist straps on and then attached them to the bar with the Velcro strips. Tommy was ordered to attempt his first set of ten.

"Good job, Tommy. You've already got a great back and awesome shoulders but this exercise in particular will help put on some more mass. That's it, now one more," he said with a laugh and a second light slap on the ass.

Tommy had imagined himself totally spent, but that slap galvanized him to struggle through one more pull-up. Exhausted after that, he dangled from the wrist straps and tried to catch his breath.

While resting, Tommy gazed into the large wall mirror in front of him. His short red hair was already plastered to his forehead with sweat, and his taut body glistened with a sheen of it. Hours in the sun had bestowed upon him a freckled tan that contrasted with the pale-yellow tank top he wore. His underarms were smooth and pale though, not receiving as much exposure as the rest of his body. He was proud of his compact build but wanted to add some bulk to it, which was why he had hired a personal trainer.

Occupied with contemplating his image, he hadn't noticed Raphael rummaging through his trainer's bag until he came up behind him again. He was rubbing his hands together, apparently working in some hand cream he had taken from his bag.

That seemed a little odd, but he didn't question it as Raphael offered him a stunning smile in the mirror and nodded. "Second set. This one will be harder than the last, I can guarantee you that."

His meaning became clear after Tommy had completed his eighth rep and was about to attempt his ninth. Abruptly, Raphael reached out and grasped the waistband of his shorts, then yanked them down to his knees.

The redhead gasped, staring open-mouthed at his image as his boner was revealed in all its pink, curved glory while Raphael chuckled behind him. But that was only the prelude to what happened next.

One of the trainer's hands thrust up into his asscrack and a finger, slippery from hand cream, found his puckered asshole. It dug past the sphincter and twisted its way inward.

With his crotch exposed and that finger unexpectedly poking up his twitching asshole, the young lifeguard's freckled complexion blushed crimson. The workout area was cavernous

with high ceilings and when Tommy emitted a little squeal as
that finger penetrated his snug sphincter, it reverberated around
the empty room. He only hoped Bradley, who was upstairs at
the front desk doing some paperwork, couldn't hear him!

"One more, Tommy," Raphael ordered, his dark eyes meeting
Tommy's blue ones in the mirror.

The lifeguard was in no position to argue. The ache of that
finger wriggling around in his butthole, the image of himself
dangling from the bar with his bare cock standing at attention
and Raphael's teasing smirk staring back at him, were a combination too powerful to ignore, or resist.

Tommy pulled himself upward, biting his lip and moaning
as that finger followed him, burying itself deeper as he rose all
the way, then began the descent. Raphael's hand in his crack felt
huge as that finger burrowed even deeper.

"Three sets in a row now, with only thirty seconds rest
between them. All out, now!"

Tommy obeyed. The Brazilian's training method was
certainly unorthodox, to say the least, but it worked magic on
his resolve to push himself beyond his limits!

That probing finger followed him up and down as he
performed rep after rep. Between sets, as he dangled breathlessly, the finger wriggled around inside him and had him
moaning and gasping for breath. In the mirror, his pink cock
jerked wildly with every wriggle and thrust of the trainer's
insinuating finger.

On the final set, as Tommy struggled upward, Raphael's
finger twisted up Tommy's ass, shoved deeper, then abruptly
pulled out. Almost immediately two fingers replaced it. "One
more?" he teased as he slowly pressed inward past a straining
sphincter and Tommy pulled himself upward on the bar, his legs
thrashing and his chest heaving.

The pair of fingers stretched his aching gut as he strained to complete that final pull-up. He did it! Then on the way down, the fingers rammed deep and twisted. He grunted like a gored pig.

"Good job, Tommy. Now time for a little rest."

Tommy quickly discovered his trainer apparently didn't mean Tommy's asshole was going to get a rest, though! Without removing the probing pair of digits, he ducked between the lifeguard's dangling legs and turned around in front of him. Smiling still, he yanked down on the redhead's shorts and pulled them the rest of the way off to toss them to the floor. He then raised one leg at a time and placed them on his shoulders. His face was in Tommy's crotch.

"Take it easy for a few minutes before we start the second part of your workout," Raphael ordered.

It was easy enough to rest in that position. Tommy gripped the bar above while the wrist straps held him up and his lower body was supported by Raphael's broad shoulders. Two fingers twisted inside his quivering hole while he inhaled deeply to get his breath back and his racing heart began to slow. But his slowing heart began to pound again as the trainer once more did the unexpected and Tommy grew even more excited.

Raphael pulled Tommy's lower body forward and stuck his face down between his thighs. Suddenly he was licking his crack! Then he pulled his fingers out of Tommy's hole and stuck his tongue inside it.

Loud slurps echoed in the quiet training room. Raphael wasn't the least bit restrained in his oral attack. He licked, sucked, and smacked his lips as he ate away. Tommy wriggled around the tongue and lips and moaned nonstop. His muscles, already exhausted from the pull-ups, were like quivering jelly and he found himself totally yielding to that oral attack. By this time, he was feeling like he could take just about anything up his hole!

That's when he spotted Bradley in the mirror. The dark-skinned desk clerk was all smiles as he watched the pair engage in the unorthodox training session. Tommy couldn't help but notice he had pushed down his shorts and was pumping the biggest black dick the redhead had ever seen.

"One more to join your session?"

Raphael heard his buddy's query and pulled out of Tommy's asscrack to respond. "Sure. Why don't you unstrap my client and we'll put him on the slanted bench to finish up his training for the night?"

Tommy didn't say a word. He was too shocked and too thrilled to risk spoiling the moment by saying anything that might halt it. Bradley was a muscle-bound hunk with a sweet personality and Tommy had always nurtured a secret crush on him. Tonight, it looked like he was getting the best workout of his life, and a piece of that huge black dick too!

They moved the compliant young stud to the slanted bench, actually carrying him between them, laughing and playfully slapping his bare butt and his twitching hard-on as they did.

He found himself planted facedown on the slanted workout bench. They cranked it up so that he was almost upright and his face was at crotch height for Bradley to move in and thrust that enormous dark cock in his mouth. He gulped it in without a word.

"Hungry boy, that's for sure," Bradley crooned, his deep voice melodic and thrilling.

As he gobbled that huge piece of meat, he felt Raphael's hands on his sides as he crouched behind him. The walls, as in most gyms, were lined with mirrors and he could see the trainer had discarded his own shorts and was naked from the waist down. His lower body was exceptional, long thighs of smooth muscle and big calves, while his ass was round and muscular, all a flawless dusky brown. His cock reared upward in a wicked curve with a foreskin that was peeled back to reveal half the drooling knob.

Tommy's ass was wide open with his feet on either side of the bench. Raphael lifted his compact butt from the seat and immediately crammed a pair of slippery fingers back up his spit-coated hole. They drove in easily—the trainer had apparently used more of the hand cream to lubricate them!

His cock followed, just as slippery with a coating of hand cream. Tommy arched his back and rammed his ass downward to envelop Raphael's hot cock with his hungry hole. The thick tool slithered inward without a hitch.

He groaned around cock, one black and one brown, swallowing as much of one with his mouth as he could and driving downward to gulp up as much of the other as he could with his quivering asslips. Out of the corner of his eye he could see what was going on in one of the wall mirrors. He was half-naked on the bench getting fucked in both ends! His freckled body, taut with muscle, was being impaled by black dick in one end while a brown cock thrust up between his white asscheeks at the other end. It looked as exciting as it felt!

"Good job, Tommy. But how about one more? How about one more cock? Can you take it? Hell, I know you can take it."

Tommy wasn't sure what the trainer meant as he was already taking two cocks, one up the ass and one in his mouth. But Bradley laughed out loud and obviously understood. Tommy for the first time began to wonder if the pair had planned this—and perhaps had done it before!

Bradley pulled out of Tommy's slurping mouth and quickly stripped down to his tennis shoes. He was glorious in his ebony nudity, broad and smooth with truly huge shoulders. Grinning and rubbing his black dick over Tommy's bright red face one more time, he then came around behind the pair on the bench. He and Raphael worked together without having to say anything. Lifting Tommy again, Raphael slid in beneath him to lie back on the slanted bench. Then they lowered Tommy over the trainer's thick brown cock.

Tommy groaned as the big tool again slithered up his gut. He still didn't know what they planned until Bradley crouched behind him and began to probe his crack with his own huge cock.

Suddenly he understood what one more cock meant!

Fortunately that monster black dick had been coated in more of Raphael's hand cream as it began to push against the puckered pink sphincter already stuffed with brown cock. Tommy shuddered all over and bit his lip with fearful anticipation. Could he take it?

"You can take it. Just take a deep breath and push outward. I know you can do it, Tommy."

Raphael gazed up into his eyes as he spoke, his engaging smile melting any final resistance on Tommy's part.

Amazingly, that second cock began to push past his butt rim and into his steamy hole. It ached, but it felt good at the same time. He did as Raphael suggested and took a deep breath, exhaled and sat down at the same time.

"Oh my fucking god," he yelped as the cockhead popped inside him and a thick black shaft began to slide in beside the one already planted deeply there.

"There's one more for you. How's that feel, dude?" Bradley said as he leaned in and crooned in his ear.

Tommy was unable to respond. Raphael had pulled his face down and planted his luscious lips over his, then immediately began to tongue-fuck his mouth. While Raphael lay back beneath him and pumped his cock upward into Tommy's straining hole and kissed him thoroughly, Bradley thrust in and out from behind him. The two wrapped their powerful arms around him and went to town on his ass.

It was all-consuming. Two cocks rubbed back and forth in his gut, stretching his asslips to their max while probing deep inside to massage his prostate in the most exciting ways. His own cock drooled and twitched between his smooth belly and Raphael's rippled abs. Bradley had pulled up their shirts so that their naked torsos could slide together. Raphael continued kissing him all the while.

The pair of cocks worked in aching rhythm for a while, then alternated as one pulled almost out, then pushed deep as the other withdrew to hover at his tenderized asslips. He couldn't hold still with all that action and began to hump and squirm between them, gurgling around Raphael's buried tongue and snorting for air. He outdid himself, grinding his flushed white ass downward and taking both cocks to the balls.

Tommy floated in a miasma of muscle and sweat and cock until he felt his orgasm rising up to abruptly overcome him. He grunted around Raphael's tongue as his cock spewed between their mashed bellies. The two cocks in his ass thrust faster all at once and he realized the other two were about to follow his example.

"Awesome hole, Tommy," Bradley crooned in his ear as he pulled out and let loose his own spray of cum.

He hosed Tommy's ivory-white butt crack as Raphael pulled out and did the same. Another jet of nut juice splattered his sweaty ass. The three of them writhed around on the bench as their balls drained and their hearts raced.

When they were finally spent, Raphael broke their kiss and smiled up at him. "I think we're done for the night, Tommy. Good work."

Tommy, somewhat shell-shocked from the totally surprising experience, blurted out the one thing no one might have expected of him.

"How about one more?"

Raphael and Bradley howled with laughter. Then they lifted him up, placed him on his back on the bench press and hooked his legs behind the bar. His battered ass and stretched pink hole were exposed and ready.

Then they proceeded to give him what he wanted. One more.

# THE ROPES

## Gregory L. Norris

He'd hated gym class from the day a phys-ed coach in green shorts barked at him to scale the rope, higher and higher. Nick was a monkey as a kid and had climbed all of the tall pines and many of the maple trees in the backyard and surrounding neighborhood, even one of the towering oaks. But the most he managed on the rope was a few feet off the shiny parquet floor. Rope wasn't branch, and it burned his wrists. His breath boiled in his lungs. After that morning, gym stopped being like recess and was no longer fun.

This gym was different. He was here by choice, and the membership was yet another perk of his new job in the city. School was over by two full years and a handful of months, and Nick Canfield wouldn't have to put up with any ridicule—or ropes. Still, memories flooded back as he toured the facility and breathed in the familiar stink of male sweat, a narcotic haze that hung over the men's locker room.

"...cardio machines and aerobics," blathered his guide, one of the gym's managers. "Spinning class if you have the raw dedication."

*The balls, in other words,* thought Nick. Oh yeah, he did.

He drew in a deep breath of the male scent that infused the men's locker room at Fit Physique, the gym in his new neighborhood just north of Boston, and tipped a glance at the nearest mirror. At twenty, the last of his baby fat was on its way out, and Nick mostly liked what he saw: neat dark hair, attractive face, and a body ready to be sculpted by regular visits. He could work out after clocking out at his new job in concert promotions, and on weekends. Nick, who didn't know a lot of people apart from work, might make some friends, pick up a workout buddy, maybe more.

A dude dressed only in a towel strutted into the locker room from the direction of the showers. The clean smell of a man's shampoo and soap, the latter likely green—a brand named in honor of Ireland—teased Nick's next breath. The man stowed his shower gear in one of the lockers.

"Hey, Cody," Nick's tour guide said.

The dude shuffled around on a pair of slides, and Nick silently drank in as much of the man's magnificence as possible. Nick's age if he had to guess, clearly an athlete—Nick had no trouble dressing him in a baseball uniform or a hoops jersey and shorts, short blond hair in a clean cut, eyes beyond simply blue. *Sapphires,* thought Nick.

"'Sup," the gym god said, a man of few words.

"Cody McClain, this is Nick, our newest member."

Cody's sapphire gemstone eyes drilled into Nick's. "Hey."

Nick boldly offered his hand. Cody hesitated. His eyes scanned Nick's outstretched fingers before committing, then accepted the gesture. Pressure clamped down on Nick's hand. With little effort, he imagined the other young man snapping his bones. From the periphery, he recorded the line of fur cutting Cody McClain down the middle of his abdomen and circling around his navel, hairy legs and big jock feet. Heavenly distraction.

The shake ended, and Cody turned back to his locker.

"If you come this way, I'll show you the rest," Nick's guide said.

Nick followed, but tipped a glance behind him in time to see Cody unhook the towel. The towel dropped and puddled around those big feet, exposing the most perfect ass Cody had ever seen—firm, high, the kind of definition that transforms ass muscles from roundness to a squarer geometry. A thin Mohawk of dark blond fur dissected the two halves down the middle. The gym god reached into his locker for something, and the perfect halves parted enough for Nick to steal a glance at the meaty balls dangling beneath, visible one instant, gone the next.

*Cody*, Nick thought. Then he choked down a swallow and discovered his mouth had gone completely dry, his throat baked to desert like on that long-ago day when he was forced to climb the rope.

He pushed himself, harder and faster, on the treadmill and the stationary bike. The weight machines and aerobic classes tested him at first but grew easier and more enjoyable as the month progressed. The aches of those first weeks subsided; muscle began to emerge. With it came a boldness beaten out of him in the gyms of his past, where the ropes mocked him.

Sweat coated Nick's flesh. He peeled off his shirt, unlaced his sneakers, and removed socks and then workout shorts. The last stitch—his nut-soaked jockstrap, black—came off his body reluctantly. Nick glanced around the men's locker room once more to be sure he was alone before raising the damp cotton to his nose. The rich odor of a man's scent filled his next deep breath.

"*Cody...fuck*," Nick whispered.

In his imagination, the stink belonged to the other young

man. The sound of the big door whooshing open and a scuffle
of footsteps on the tiled floor alerted Nick to the presence of
approaching eyes. He stuffed the jock into the locker with the
rest of his workout gear and wrapped a towel around his waist.

A guilty glance to his right, and Cody McClain jumped out
of Nick's mind and into real time.

"Dude," Cody said.

A shiver tripped down Nick's spine, one curiously hotter
than chilly. "Hey, man."

That was it, their exchange a paltry handful of words. From
the cut of his eye, Nick watched Cody fiddle with his phone and
then strip down from T-shirt and jeans, all the while pretending
to be busy with the things inside his open locker. Cody's shirt
came off, baring spine. Belt unbuckled, zipper unzipped, Cody's
jeans fell to his ankles, showing the gray boxer-briefs spray-
painted over that incredible ass, which Nick had fantasized over
nonstop for weeks.

Cody stepped out of his kicks. Pants came off, shorts went
on. A different shirt for working out—a navy-blue tank that
accentuated Cody's amazing sapphire gaze while showing off
the nests of dark fur under his armpits.

Nick's next breath jammed halfway down his throat. For a
tense moment, all he could think about was burying his nose
in all that hair, inhaling until he got high. Cody's pits first,
and then working his way down to the dude's toes, sniffing the
sweaty cotton of his socks. Back up, but only as far as the gym
god's nut sac. The final prize was the dude's ass. Oh, to shove
his face between those firm, square halves, to lick and keep on
licking until—

Cody turned around and faced Nick. Nick froze under the
intense scrutiny of the young man's gaze. He'd been caught
staring, *lusting*, Nick was sure. Adding to his misery was
the realization that he'd gotten hard from sniffing Imaginary

Cody's potent ball-stink and from ogling Real-Time Cody with his glances.

"I want to ask you something," said the true version.

Nick found his voice. "Sure," he managed, though he expected to look down and see his dick had poked its way through the gap in his towel, condemning him fully.

Cody's mouth softened into the closest thing to a smile Nick had seen since joining Fit Physique. "I heard you're a big-league concert promoter."

Nick snorted a laugh. "Not exactly—I work in ticket sales."

Cody fumbled the meaty fullness at the front of his shorts. "Really, dude. Think you can do me a solid?"

"Maybe. What do you need?"

"Hook me up with tickets to Blindman's Bluff. I hear they're coming to town for the Blinders tour."

"Yeah, they're playing at the Atlantic Commons. I'll see what I can do," Nick said.

Cody marched over and extended his fist, knuckles aimed at Nick for a knock. "Fucking sweet, dude."

Real cool, Nick punched knuckles with the gym god, his cock at its hardest concealed by his towel.

"You finished?" Cody asked.

"Yeah, just wrapped up—gonna grab a shower before I bounce."

"Maybe next time we can meet up and workout together. Buddy up. If you want."

If Nick wanted? A hundred images flashed through the forefront of his mind's eye, rapid-fire. Before he could respond, Cody about-faced, leaving Nick standing with a boner barely under cover.

Facing the wall, he lathered up. Nick was the only man in the showers, though he doubted the situation would differ much

pounds of solid metal ruled by 170 pounds of male muscle. "Yeah," he exhaled.

His breath stirred the heady smell of a man's athletic sweat. Nick's mind again wandered. How would it be between Cody's legs? Hot and damp from the rewards of their intense workout. His asshole, right now, too. Nick dreamed of his tongue licking behind Cody's hairy nuts, seeking the fur-ringed bullet hole at the center of his butt halves. Nick's next sip of air came with difficulty.

"What about them?" Cody pressed. "The ropes?"

"Like Davis Lancaster, I guess. The ropes were my version of an obstacle to overcome."

Cody lifted the weights. "I get it. So now it's your turn to face your enemy and lift, dude."

They switched positions, with Nick on the bench gazing up instead of down at Cody's handsome face.

"You can do it," the gym god urged.

Nick pushed with his arm muscles, aware of the pressure to perform, the temptation to glance at the prominent bulge hanging down the front of Cody's shorts.

"Don't worry about it, dude," said Cody. "We all have blind spots. We all got our fucking ropes."

Their eyes connected. For a startling instant, Nick fell into the sapphire gravity overhead, convinced that he could read Cody's secret thoughts. He understood the look of desire staring back, and the way Cody's throat knotted under the influence of a heavy swallow. Nick's cock pulsed. If he dared look, he expected Cody's would be hard and leaking, too, close enough to kiss.

Then Cody blinked, and the hard edge returned to his expression.

"Come on, nut up, dude," Cody growled. "Lift those fucking weights!"

* * *

Nick secured a pair of tickets, as requested, third row center. Excellent seats, at his company discount. He handed Cody the envelope with the printouts.

Cody handed back cash. "Thanks, bro."

"No problem. Anything for my workout buddy," Nick said.

Cody closed the gym locker. "Anything?"

The long word instantly dialed up the temperature. Cody's twin sapphire eyes locked on to his. Nick attempted to answer, but opening his mouth took the greatest effort.

"S-sure," he stammered.

Cody opened the envelope. "Good, then come with me to Blindman's Bluff."

The gym god extended one of the tickets. Nick reached a trembling hand out and accepted.

Would he do anything for Cody McClain?

Nick closed his eyes, reached down and found his cock stiff in his underwear. "Fuck," he sighed.

After a few rough fumbles, he pulled his fingers off the prize and focused on the day's most pressing business. Blindman's Bluff had capitalized on the popular scruffster's look, a laid-back, casual image, the modern-day version of grunge. He chose decent jeans and sneakers and a black short-sleeved T-shirt, which he'd wear over a long-sleeved, white. The ensemble looked fresh in his imagination, especially given the toned appearance of his body after months of working out.

Nick felt excited about the night, but also anxious. His thoughts returned to Cody. His right hand skipped back down his chest and settled on familiar territory. He'd look amazing in those clothes, sure. But all he could focus on was Cody, sans his. Beating off was not only inevitable, it was necessary. Cody had offered to drive them into the city for the concert. Nick would never make it through the night without some strategic relief. He tipped a glance at the clock on his phone—still plenty of time to rub one out before the arrival of the star of his fantasies.

A knock sounded on the apartment's front door. Nick groaned and swore beneath his breath, contemplated ignoring his surprise visitor but then reached for the jeans. He pulled them on en route to the front door and suffered his erection's complaints while stuffing it under cover.

Nick opened the door. Fresh, warm air spilled into the apartment, along with a cascade of golden afternoon sunlight. Somewhere in that effulgence stood a form, impressive in height and physique. Nick blinked, and a gym god stepped out of the sunshine.

"Dude," said Cody.

Nick flashed a wide, nervous smile. "Hey, you're not due for—"

"I know," said Cody.

Confusion challenged Nick's happiness. For a terrible instant, he worried some problem had arisen, that the concert at the Atlantic Commons was off.

"Is something wrong?"

Cody's eyes narrowed. "No, not really. Yeah, dude. I don't fucking know."

Nick drank in the vision before him: a scruffster clad in jeans, T-shirt, and old boots that loved his body. Cody also wore a baseball cap, its bill aimed forward. A young man with a much older man's sapphire gemstone eyes shifted from one foot to the other, his body language impossible to misread.

"Come on in," Nick said.

Cody hesitated. Then he followed Nick inside, out of the sunshine. Once the door closed, Cody seized hold of Nick's face in both hands. Nick froze. Unable to look away, Nick again greeted Cody's eyes directly.

"The ropes," Cody said.

And then he pressed his mouth awkwardly against Nick's. Nick's arms shot out, his paralysis broken. The kiss ended.

"Dude, if you're done with me..."

Nick found his voice and said, "I'm not."

"I'm so sorry."

"Fuck, dude, don't be."

Nick moved forward and reestablished the kiss. This time, their mouths locked. Lips softened. Tongues joined in. The sun-warmed cotton of Cody's shirt brushed Nick's bare chest, unleashing concentric waves that aroused his nipples into hard points. Boldly, he reached lower.

*A dream*, thought Nick. He was still in his bedroom, his dick hanging out, lubed with spit. Only the heat radiating up from Cody's cock into his fingertips was real, not fantasy.

"Nick," growled Cody during a breath for breath, "I haven't stopped thinking about you since we met."

Nick nodded. "Me, too. If you knew how much, how badly, I've wanted you."

Cody flashed a smile. "I can guess."

Nick groped the gym god's bulge. Cody was hard, too, and pressed into his palm.

"Oh, fuck, dude—we gonna do this?" asked Cody.

"We got more than enough time before the concert," said Nick. "Fuck those ropes."

He worked a finger into Cody's belt and guided the gym god into the bedroom.

# MEANS TO
# AN END

## Rob Rosen

Night janitor. It's what my world was reduced to. Times, after all, were hard, but the men at the gym were even harder. So, yeah, my McJob had its perks. Best of all, I got there just before the place closed, so everyone that remained was in the locker room: getting dressed, getting in the shower or out, toweling off, and any other assorted activities that involved them being naked and me ogling while presumably cleaning.

As for me, well now, me they ignored. Fine, I could live with that. It made it easier, after all, to sidle by unnoticed and stare at their broad expanses of chests and backs, at muscle-dense thighs and perfect asses, at dangling balls and swaying pricks. It was a veritable sea of naked flesh, all mine to swim in, even if my backstroke was done by my eyes alone.

Still, to be honest, this was better than Internet porn. This was up close and personal, dozens upon dozens of men for my mind to catalog, images to use at a later time to jack off to. Heck, once everyone was gone, I could do all the jacking I liked. And—guess what?—I liked. Go figure.

Plus, lots of them left their dirty clothes behind, sweat-soaked T-shirts to use the next day, towels too, and socks. Though my favorite, by far, were the jockstraps and boxers and white cotton briefs, all smelling of musk and sweat and sex: a heady aroma to be sure.

And with me naked, my mop off to the side, I could sniff and stroke to my heart's content, remembering the man who'd worn the clothes just a short while earlier, my come building all the while, eyelids fluttering, balls bouncing on the wooden bench before I shot and shot and shot some more. Bitter irony: then I had to clean it all up. No biggie; I could live with that, could spew from night to night, a different pair of shorts wedged beneath my nose each time. Honestly, there were worse things.

Though by far the worst was the fact that, though I knew these men intimately, knew their bodies, their dicks and asses, their scents, I could never have any of them firsthand. Because while they were leaving, to get on with their lives, I was left at the gym, hours later, cleaning and scrubbing and mopping and dusting—that is when I wasn't coming.

There was this one guy who really set my bells and whistles off. He worked out a few nights a week, same schedule, always naked at the exact same time in front of the exact same locker. Now he, he was my sole regret, the one I wish I could've met, could've talked to besides the barely muttered, "Hey," as me and my mop bucket quickly slid past.

Dude was about the same age as me, late twenties, maybe early thirties at most. He was shorter than me by an inch or two, but broader by far, packed with muscle, all of it covered in a fine, brown down. Oh, but it was those eyes of his, eyes so blue you could just about take a dip in them; now they were hard to ignore, hard to walk by.

They were, in fact, hard not to get hard over.

His locker was the one I usually visited first, once everyone was gone and I was left to my own devices. More often than not, he never locked it. After all, there was nothing in there worth stealing. Not unless you had a hankering for sweaty, used tighty-whities, which, of course, I always did.

Got to be all I had to do was look at that locker and my cock was suddenly hard as granite. Then I'd strip naked, fifth limb of a prick swaying as I drew nearer, heartbeat double-timing as my hand reached for the handle. Up it went, the metal clicking. It was the only other sound in the locker room besides my heavy panting.

Same thing happened on that one fateful night, me naked, the locker opened, my eyes glued, locked and stapled to the contents. *"Fuuuck,"* I rasped, hand on the prize: white briefs, still moist, still smelling of his sweaty cock and balls, a few strands of curly black pubes left as a consolation prize for yours truly.

Down I sat, the wood cold and smooth on my ass. His underwear was gripped tight in my hand, stuffed beneath my nose, cotton brushing my lips. I took a deep whiff, my cock throbbing in my grasp, precome seeping from the tip, balls already tight. Dude didn't smell like all the rest of them. There was something else there, something exotic, like a fruit from a faraway land you've only ever seen in a magazine. And damn if I didn't want to pick that fucking fruit, to take a mighty chomp out of it.

Instead, I settled for its scent, wisps of it falling around my head, making me dizzy as I jacked furiously away at my prick. I took another deep draw from the undies, another, another, the come welling up with each sharp inhale. At last, with a feral haze of his magnificent stink swirling around my head, my cock erupted, a mighty stream of spunk splitting the air before raining down in great, white gobs of pearlescent spooge before landing in muffled splats on the tiled floor below.

I grinned at the mess I'd made as I sat there trying to catch my breath. "Clean up in aisle two," I rasped. I then watched my cock shrink, a last drop of come dripping to the floor, before I stood up and placed his underwear back in the locker.

It was then that I spotted it. "A ring," I whispered. "He must've put it in here and forgotten about it." I carefully removed it. Thing was all gold, expensive looking. I started to put it back, then had second thoughts. Nope, I wasn't stealing it. Times were hard, but not that hard. Instead, I was going to use it: a means to an end.

See, all kinds of things got lost in that gym, all kinds of things misplaced, dropped, left behind. In fact, we had ourselves quite a packed lost and found hamper and a crammed bulletin board with notes from people looking for any number of items they thought they had lost while working out.

I smiled as I pocketed the ring. It was safe, for the time being. Safe, that is, until he went looking for it.

The note appeared two days later. The ring was described to a T. Thing even had a reward, but I had other things besides money on my mind. He left an email address on the poster. I contacted him as soon as the gym closed and told him I thought I might've found his treasured ring and to drop by the gym later that night to pick it up. I even sent him a pic of it. Suffice to say, he was eager to connect with me. Suffice to say, that made two of us.

A couple of hours later, the night sky dark, I heard a knock on the front door. My heart skipped a beat, belly suddenly in knots, a trickle of sweat beelining down my face. I walked to the door and peeked through the slats. I grinned when I recognized him. *Bingo.*

I unlocked the door and let him inside. "Um, hi," I managed to squeak out.

He smiled and nodded. "Thank god you found it. Where was it?"

I closed the door behind us, my pants tight around the crotch all of a sudden. "Beneath the lockers. Must've rolled there," I told him. "I was sweeping when it came rolling back out." I held my hand out. "Ben."

His nod returned, the smile a tad brighter. "Paul. And thanks," he said, his hand in mine, flesh on glorious flesh, my cock swelling even more upon impact. "Can I, um, have it back now?"

I coughed. "Oh, uh, sure," I sputtered. "Follow me."

Through the gym we strode, quickly arriving in the locker room. Just him and me. Alone. I could actually hear my heart pounding now, my dick ready to explode. Here he finally was. And then we were in the manager's office and I was handing him the ring.

He breathed a sigh of relief. "It was my dad's. I would've killed myself if I lost it." And, yes, I almost felt guilty. Almost. But there he was, and there were those eyes of his, sparkling like sapphires beneath the fluorescent lights, and guilt was the last thing I was feeling. He then reached inside and removed his wallet. Out came three crisp twenties. "Here. Please, take it. And thanks again."

I shook my head. "That's not what I want."

He paused. Perhaps he caught the edge to my voice. Perhaps it was my odd choice of wording, the hidden implication that I did in fact want something from him. Our eyes suddenly locked, all that blue blocking out everything else. For a moment he paused yet again, until the smile returned to his handsome face.

"Weird being here at night," he said. Ironically, for me, it was only weird not being there at night. "I mean, it's so quiet now. Empty. No lockers slamming, no keys jangling, no, um, naked dudes."

It was the way he said that last part that made me gulp. "Not right now, no," I said, my voice thick, raspy.

A flush of red worked its way up his neck. He turned and walked the twenty feet or so to the rear of the locker room. Back there was the sauna, the hot tub, the steam room. "You, uh, you use these once everyone is gone?"

I shrugged. "Sometimes," I replied, now standing just a couple of inches away from him. "Mostly, I just clean up and try to get the hell out of here." It was now my turn to pause, a nervousness pushing through me that made my legs shake. "You...you want to go in?"

He turned, his face even closer now, close enough to smell his sweet breath. "In the hot tub?" He looked from me to it and back again. "Has been a long day. Might be nice."

My smile returned. And, no, I didn't give him a chance to change his mind. Meaning, I kicked my sneakers off and shimmied out of my work duds before he could even untie his shoelaces, leaving me in my socks and boxers, which were now tenting something fierce.

"Long day," I replied. "Um, yeah."

He eyed me, taking me in as he removed his shoes. "You work out," he made note, pointing north to south.

I nodded. "Well, I do have easy access." I pointed at him, south to north, in return as his northern regions started coming into view, dense pecs revealed, a forest of chest chair. "Obviously, so do you."

His shirt was laid over a nearby bench, his belt buckle unbuckled, zipper slipped down. My gulp returned. "I try to." His slacks slid off, leaving him in dress socks and tenting briefs—briefs, in fact, that I knew all too well, said pair registering in my mind's eye almost immediately, the intoxicating scent remembered, my cock pulsing at the mere thought.

"It shows," I said, voice fairly trembling.

He stared at my crotch, then down at his own. "Seems like lots of things are showing."

I nodded. "Or are about to."

I slid out of my socks. He slid out of his. Hands shaking, heart jackrabbit fast, I pushed off my boxers, my cock swaying to and fro as I righted myself. He stared at me and then mimicked the maneuver. I'd only ever seen his cock flaccid before. Erect, it was a thing of beauty, short and thick with a fat mushroom head, balls so low they were practically in their own zip code.

"This the reward you wanted, Ben?" he asked as he slowly stepped into the hot tub, legs submerged, cock horizontal above the swirling, churning water.

I stared down at him and then joined him inside, sloshing about as I sat on one of the benches. "Better than cash, no?"

He sat on a bench across from me, his feet suddenly playing with mine. "No," he replied. "I mean, um, yes, better." His big toe pressed against my big toe. "*Much* better."

I stared across the water at him, his eyes sparkling now, bluer by far than the water we were submerged in. He grinned as he pushed himself off the bench. I grinned in return as I spread my legs wide, his body quickly kneeling in front of my body as he gazed up and I gazed down. At long last our lips met, which is about as close to landing on a cloud as a guy could get.

"Finally," I groaned.

He pulled his lips an inch away. "Finally?" He chuckled. His hand reached up and grabbed my floating prick. He gave it a squeeze, and yet another groan pushed up from my lungs. "You, uh, you wanted to do this before tonight?"

I nodded. "Every Monday, Wednesday and Friday at a quarter after seven."

He squinted his eyes shut and was clearly picturing what he was usually doing at those specific times. "That's when I'm done working out, when I'm changing to go back home. You noticed me then?"

And still I nodded. "Hard, no pun intended, not to notice."

He didn't seem to mind my admission. In fact, he was kissing me again a moment later, his hard body pressed into mine, our cocks grinding together. When he at last pulled slightly away, he asked, "Just out of curiosity, Ben, what else did you fantasize about doing with me?"

"You, um, you really want to know that?" My heart raced yet again, fast enough to post a fairly decent time at the Indy 500.

He nodded. "Please, enlighten me."

He released my prick and floated back to the other side of the hot tub. I grinned, nervously. It was, after all, one thing to imagine it (repeatedly and often), but it was another thing entirely to say it out loud to the person you've been fantasizing about.

I swallowed hard, then replied, "I'd like to sniff your asshole."

He laughed, then choked, then splashed me with water. "You're joking."

I shook my head. "Nope. That about covers it." I splashed him back. "I'd really like to sniff your ass. If that's, um, okay with you, I mean."

He shrugged, one last wave of water hitting me before he hopped up, shook off, and climbed out. I gazed in rapt delight as he just as quickly got on all fours, his feet up against the edge of the tub, ass jutting out, hole winking my way. "Sniff away, my good man."

He grabbed his cheeks and spread them wider, balls swaying, cock hovering. Reverently, I moved over and leaned in. And there it was, his beautiful asshole: hair-rimmed, pink, and puckered. Finally, my means had met his stupendous end. I breathed in deeply, eyelids fluttering as his all-too-familiar scent swirled around inside my nasal cavity. Even mixed with the chlorine, it was uniquely his, so beautiful, so unusual.

"Why do you smell like that?" I couldn't help but ask.

"Like what?" he replied, neck craned around my way.

Again I breathed in, my cock very nearly ready to explode as I did so. "Different somehow. Not so much musky as, well, spicy, woodsy, maybe with a hint of something floral." I took a hungry lick and suck and slurp of his remarkable hole. "You even taste that way, Paul. How is that possible?"

"The truth?"

I nodded and took another lap around his track, tongue delving dead center as I furiously stroked my cock, my body only knee-deep in the water now. "Please."

He shoved his ass into my face and began jacking merrily away on his thick tool. "I sweat a lot, Ben."

I shoved a spit-slick finger deep, deep, *deep* inside of him. His back arched, a loud moan instantly bouncing off the nearby lockers. "And?"

He laughed as he beat his meat, his balls swaying in time to his pounding fist and my pounding index finger. "Old Spice, Ben," he admitted with a grunt. "It's not just for armpits."

And then I laughed. All this time I thought it was something exotic, and all it was, was a bit of deodorant. I laughed again, balls raising now, his and mine both. "You're certainly getting your money's worth then, Paul."

"Really?" he groaned. "My asshole smells clean and fresh?"

I nodded, a second finger joining the fray, a third, all three working their way to his farthest reaches. "Old, no, spicy, yes. Uniquely you, Jack. Perfect, in fact." I retracted my fingers. They came out in an audible *pop*. "Now roll over, please; I want to watch you come."

"Ditto," he replied before rolling over onto his back, fat prick aimed at the ceiling, heavy balls brushing the tiled floor.

I hawked a loogie at my fingers as he again spread his meaty thighs for me, asshole quickly revealed. In they went, a sigh escaping from between his full lips, his cock again in his hand.

I then started pumping away, both on my steely prick and his stellar hole, his back arching off the floor as I fucked his rump silly with my triple digits.

"Close," he soon groaned, muscle-dense chest rapidly expanding and contracting.

"Closer," I panted back, eyes glued to his blur of a cock, watching, waiting for the inevitable.

And then he shot, thick bands of aromatic come that whooshed up before raining back down, dousing his belly in white, hot gobs of spunk. At the sight of it, at the smell of it, my own cock erupted, a lava flow of come that joined with his before splashing down to the tile below.

I huffed while he puffed, and both of us locked eyes again. All I saw was blue. Blue on top of blue. "Beautiful," I absent-mindedly whispered.

He wiped his fingers through the gooey mess of come on his belly. "I'll say."

His back went vertical while I leaned in. This kiss was even more spectacular than all the ones before it. "Can I ask a favor, Paul?"

He chuckled. "Anything you want, Ben."

I tickled his balls. "Can you, um, sort of leave your underwear here when you go?"

"Eager to get rid of me?"

I shook my head. "Not even close."

He moved his face an inch in reverse and stared into my eyes again. Suddenly, I knew what a deer felt like when the headlights were coming straight for it. "I have an entire hamper full back at my house, Ben."

I groaned at the very thought. "I get off in a few hours, Paul." I glanced down at the mess we'd made. "Plus a few minutes."

"And I'll be home in a few hours," he gleefully informed. "Want me to break out the Old Spice?"

"Nah," I replied, the kiss repeated, deep and soulful and perfect in every way. "Either way, I have a feeling I'm going to love the way you smell."

And, oh boy, did I ever.

# HELPING RUFUS

## Bob Vickery

When I told Daddy I was going out for the high school wrestling team, I could tell he wasn't pleased. He just stood there, chopping onions, the knife whacking into the cutting board so hard I thought he'd lose a finger for sure. Finally, he looked up at me, his eyes red and angry from all those onion fumes. "Who's goin' to help me out in the diner, Rufus, if you're spending all your time wrestling with your buddies after school?"

"I'll help you out after practice, Daddy. I'll still have time." Cora and Tammy were making a big deal about cleaning the counter and setting out the forks and knives. But I could tell they were listening to every word. It was too early for customers and they didn't seem to have nothin' better to do with their time.

Daddy just shook his head and started in on the peppers. "I don't know. It just don't seem like a good idea." He put the knife down and looked at me again. "How you know you'll be any good at it anyway?"

"Hell, Daddy, I'm the biggest kid in the senior class." And I am. I'm six foot three and weigh 218 pounds, stripped naked. And it's all solid too; there ain't a butcher's ounce of fat on me. I know that sounds like bragging, but it ain't. I'm just stating a fact.

Daddy snorted. "Yeah, you're the biggest kid all right. Staying back two years sure took care of that." I felt my face burn on that one, but I didn't say nothing. I just stood there watchin' Daddy have at those peppers with the cleaver like they was his worst enemy in all the world. I could tell he was ashamed for what he said by the way his mouth got all tight and his eyes squinty. That wasn't no help for me, though, 'cause when Daddy gets shamed, he just gets meaner. "You're big, all right, Rufus, but you're slow and clumsy. You need to be quick, to be a good wrestler."

"Oh, hell, George," Cora said, "If Bigfoot wants to join the wrestling team, why don't you just let him? It's only natural for a boy to want to participate in high school sports." People call me Bigfoot because I wear a size fourteen shoe and there was once a story in one of the supermarket papers about some hunters tracking Bigfoot in California. Some of the guys in school started joking about calling those hunters up and tellin' them to high-foot it over here to Enid, Oklahoma, if they really want to bag Bigfoot, and the name just sorta took.

"Yeah," Tammy laughed. "And he can practice his holds on us anytime." Cora giggled. Cora and Tammy are always making little jokes like that about me. I wish they wouldn't; it's embarrassing.

Daddy glowered at them. "I got three things to tell you ladies, no make that four. One, I don't recall asking for your opinion in this private conversation between me and my son. Two, the boy's name is Rufus. Three, I don't like you making those sexy remarks about Rufus, and four, if you can't find something better to do with your time than cackle like a couple of hens, then what the hell am I paying you for?" But Cora and Tammy just rolled their eyes and went back to wiping the counter.

Daddy threw the cleaver down on the cutting board and walked away. "Hell, Rufus, join the damn team, if that's what you want," he grunted. "You're going to anyway, whether I say so or not." And he stomped out of the kitchen and up the stairs.

Tammy came around the counter and stood next to me. "Bigfoot, would you hand me those dishes on the top shelf?" she asked me. When I reached up for them, she pressed her body tight against mine. "Just don't let those boys mess up that pretty face of yours, Bigfoot," she growled. "You're the best-looking thing this podunk town's got going for it." I didn't know what to do but just hand the plates to her. Tammy laughed. "What the hell do I want those for?" she said and walked off.

So that's how I wound up going to Coach Garibaldi and telling him I wanted to join the team. Coach just looked me over slowly, nodded, and said, "Okay, Rufus. I'll give you a try. Practice starts today after school."

I went to practice every day, and I tried real hard to learn the moves. At first, nobody wanted to wrestle me because of my size, but then some of the bigger boys took me on. And they found they could win, more often than not. I hate to say it, but Daddy was right, I am slow. And clumsy. Sometimes if I could just get a good grip on the guy, I could hold on and pin him to the mat. But if he slipped out of my hands and started his moves on me, I was a goner. I went to a few meets and usually wound up "eating mat." I was just glad that Daddy never went and saw it. I'd never hear the end of it.

Every afternoon, after practice, we all would shower up before going home. More often than not, Coach Garibaldi just stood at the doorway, sometimes talking to the other boys, giving them pointers, sometimes just watching us. Coach never much talked to me, but lately I'd begun to catch him looking at me more and more. Probably just wonderin' what to do with such a pitiful wrestler. One day, as we were all walking out of the shower back toward the lockers, he grunted and said, "I guess it's true what they say about guys with big feet." And he walked back to his office. A couple of other guys nearby laughed.

"What did Coach mean by that?" I asked.

One of the guys shook his head. "Nothin', Bigfoot."

Another guy grinned. "It's just Mother Nature's way of evening the score. You may have been behind the door when she gave out the brains, Bigfoot, but good god almighty; you sure were first in line on other days." And they laughed again and walked off. Damn fools, I thought. But it always bothers me when people won't explain a joke to me. It's not my fault I'm dumb.

I got dressed and started walking out of the locker room. When I passed Coach's office, I could see that his door was open. I heard him call my name out, and I stuck my head in. "Yeah, Coach?" I asked.

Coach was sitting behind his desk. "Come in here, Rufus," he said. Except for Daddy, Coach was the only person who called me by my Christian name. I walked in. "Close the door," he said.

I'm in for it now, I thought. When Coach asks you to close the door, you know he means business. I 'magined I was going to get a chewing out for being such a poor wrestler.

But Coach didn't look mad. In fact, he didn't look much of anything. He just sat there, leaning back on his chair, looking at me with a blank face. He finally sighed. "Rufus," he said. "I just don't know what to do with you."

I felt my face turning red. I wish that wouldn't happen all the time, but I ain't got no control over it. Daddy likes to say, laughin', "It don't take much more than a fart or a hiccup to get that boy's face as red as a baboon's ass," and he's right. Anyway, I just stood there, shiftin' from one foot to the other, feeling my face all heated up. Coach didn't say nothing more for a while, making it worse. He just sat there, his fingertips tapping together, looking straight at me. I felt like one of them bugs my cousin Olaf used to pin to a roof shingle, not enough to kill, just to get it squirming. Finally Coach cleared his throat.

"How old are you, Rufus?" he asked.

"Eighteen, Coach."

"Eighteen," Coach repeated this like it was a remarkable thing. "I'm thirty-three." He laughed. "I know to you that must sound older than dirt, but believe it or not, it just seems like yesterday that I was your age."

"Yes, Coach," I mumbled. Hell, I didn't know what else to say.

"I've been giving your case a lot of thought," Coach said. "You know what I think your problem is?"

I looked at him. "No, sir."

"It's sexual tension, Rufus. Do you know what that means?" I shook my head. "Rufus," Coach said. "Didn't your Daddy ever tell you about sex?"

Well, I just liked to die right there. I knew that by the way my face felt, it must've been redder than a damn fire engine. I shook my head, but couldn't say nothin'.

Coach smiled. "There's no reason for you to be embarrassed, son. Sex is a natural, God-given gift. But it can cause problems too, especially for young men. Now I don't mean any disrespect to your father, but he should have explained this all to you. If a young man can't find some kind of release for his sexual tension, it can affect the quality of his athletic performance. Do you understand what I'm saying, Rufus?"

I shook my head again. "Not really, Coach."

Coach sighed. "Well, it looks like I got no choice but to show you, Rufus. Lock the door."

I looked at him all surprised-like, but finally did as he said.

Coach smiled. "You're a good boy, Rufus. And believe it or not, I think you've got the makings of a damn fine athlete. But we just got to lick this sexual tension problem of yours. Now drop your pants."

Well, you could have hit me on the head with a two-by-four! "Wh-what, Coach?" I stammered.

"I said drop your pants." When I didn't do nothin', Coach made a face. "Rufus," he said, his voice all exasperated. "I've seen you in the shower dozens of times. It's not like you're showing me anything new, you know. I just want to prove a point to you." I still didn't do nothin'. "Drop 'em, Rufus!" Coach barked, and I knew there was no arguing the matter. I pulled down my blue jeans. "The underpants too," Coach said. I pulled them down to my ankles.

Coach just leaned back in his chair and looked at me—or rather, at my dick. He was wearing the funniest look I ever saw on another man's face. "Sweet Jesus in Heaven," he said, all low-like. I didn't have a Chinaman's clue as to what he was thinkin', but something in his look made my stomach flutter, like it did last summer on the Winotchka Bridge, when all the guys were daring me to jump off, and I was looking straight down into the water, trying to work up the nerve. To my embarrassment, I felt my dick start getting hard. I put my hands over it to hide this from Coach.

"Leave your hands at your sides," Coach said quietly.

I did like he told me. My dick just kept on getting harder and harder. Soon it was sticking straight out. I snuck a quick peek down at it. Sure enough, it was just as red as I knew my face must be.

Coach looked in my eyes now, all triumphant. "Do you see what I mean, Rufus?" he asked. "This proves my point exactly!"

"No, Coach. I can't say that I do."

Coach got up and walked around the desk. He stood right in front of me. I was a good three inches taller than him, so he had to look up into my face. "Rufus," he said. "You've got the biggest cock I've ever seen. Hell, it must be at least ten, maybe eleven inches long." He reached down and grabbed it. "Look, I can hardly put my hand around it. With a cock like that, a man's just got to be full of sexual tension. He can't help but think of nothing but where to put this pecker. And look how easy it was for you to get hard. No wonder you can't put your mind on your athletic performance!"

Well, I just felt lower than a snake's belly in a wagon rut hearing this. 'Cause I knew Coach was right. Even now, pert near all I could think of was how good Coach's hand felt wrapped around my dick. And here Coach was just trying to prove a point. Coach was so wrapped up in makin' his point, though, that he must not have noticed that his hand was slowly stroking my dick up and down. But I sure knew it. And what's worse, I didn't want him to stop. "I'm sorry, Coach," I said, all low and sad-like.

Coach smiled. He reached up and squeezed my shoulder. He also squeezed my dick in the same friendly way. "Hell, Rufus," he said. "It's nothing to apologize for. Lots of young men suffer from sexual tension. Some of my most promising athletes. I see it as part of my job as a coach to help them through the problem."

I'll be darned if my eyes didn't start watering up when he said that. Coach was taking such an open-hearted concern in helping me through this "sexual tension" problem that it just choked me up. "What are we going to do, Coach?" I asked.

Coach smiled again, and it was such a friendly, encouraging smile, that I couldn't help but take heart. "Well, Rufus," he said, "we're just going to have to explore the problem, find out just what causes this sexual tension to flare up, and then work it through. Now take off the rest of your clothes."

# HEART ON

## Michael Bracken

The scrubs worn by the staff and the average age of the people using the exercise equipment made the medical center's cardiopulmonary rehabilitation center nothing but a high-priced gym with short-term memberships paid for by various health insurance plans. In my early fifties, I was younger than most of the other patients, but that didn't make me any healthier. Only a few weeks earlier, after decades of inadequate exercise and poor dietary habits, I had undergone quadruple heart-bypass surgery. Following surgery my cardiologist had prescribed—in fact, had demanded—my participation in rehab.

Other than the occasional use of hotel fitness centers while traveling for business, I had not been inside a gym of any kind since college, so when I first shuffled in I was unprepared for the number and variety of fitness machines filling the rehab center. Treadmills lined one wall; stationary and recumbent bicycles lined another, and arranged throughout the remaining space in some pattern that I could not fathom were various weight machines and equipment that I could not identify at first glance.

The physical therapist assigned to my case—a hot little number in his midthirties who would have made my cock rise under other circumstances—took me into a private room where he weighed me, measured me and discussed my cardiologist's rehabilitation plan. As we talked, he attached a trio of electrodes to my chest, sticking them where my hair was only beginning to regrow. Wires from the electrodes trailed under my shirt to a transmitter that hung from my belt and sent data about my heart to an EKG at the nurse's station in the center of the outer equipment room.

Then he led me out of the private room, stuck me on a treadmill set to the slowest speed and walked away. I could barely keep up and I stopped the treadmill after a few minutes.

Trevor noticed my distress and hurried to my side. He helped me to a nearby chair. "You're already out of breath."

"You," I said with a wink, "take my breath away."

He laughed and patted my hand. "You're in no condition to make passes, Mr. Tate."

"Call me Bob," I said. "And if I was?"

When he leaned forward and whispered in my ear, my physical therapist provided a workout incentive that I had not anticipated when I'd shuffled into the rehab center an hour earlier. "I'd fuck you so hard your heart would break the EKG."

"Is that a promise?"

"Get well," Trevor said as he straightened, "and we'll see what happens."

An elderly woman was struggling on one of the stationary bicycles so Trevor left me sitting in the chair while he attended to her needs. I watched him work with the woman. Even the loose-fitting blue scrubs couldn't hide the classic V of his figure—broad shoulders, thick chest, narrow waist, and tight ass held aloft on muscular legs—nor could it hide the tantalizing bulge of his personal exercise equipment.

I remembered when just the thought of unwrapping the package of a man like Trevor would have given me serious wood and weeks of masturbation fantasies, but as I sat watching him work with the woman my cock didn't even twitch once. I had not noticed any significant diminishing of sexual performance prior to heart surgery, so I didn't know if the lack of response to Trevor's sex appeal was a cardiovascular problem or a side effect of all the drugs pumping through my body.

Trevor was back at my side before I had time to overthink the cause of my dangling dick. With his help, I returned to the treadmill for a few minutes more but I didn't do much else during my first visit to the rehab center.

"I want you to strut out of here when you finish rehab," Trevor said during my second visit as he attached the electrodes to my chest before my workout, "looking and feeling better than you have in years."

Though his fingers did not linger and he didn't act in any way that might be considered unprofessional, I appreciated Trevor's touch. My previous relationship had ended almost a year before my surgery and the last two men to touch my chest had been the one who broke my heart and the one who cracked my chest to put it back together. "I bet you say that to all your patients."

"Of course I do," he said, "but with you I mean it. Take a look around. With most of these people I'm just trying to ensure they can take care of themselves when their insurance benefits expire. I'm expecting something more from you."

"A broken EKG?"

He smiled as he switched on the transmitter hanging from my belt. "But not today."

I had not considered myself out of shape prior to my surgery, but clearly I was. The purpose of rehab was to increase both my stamina and my strength, and I spent most of my first few visits shuffling along on the treadmill. Then Trevor started me on the weight machines and gave me exercises I could do at home with two-pound free weights. Over the next few visits, when he wasn't flirting with me, he slowly increased the treadmill speed and the treadmill incline, just as he slowly increased the weight I lifted on the weight machines. After several weeks I realized that my body had changed and was still changing. Not only was I able to walk longer distances at higher speeds without losing my breath, my pants were looser and my sleeves tighter around my biceps. Though my weight barely changed, fat was morphing into muscle.

Just as important—to me, at least—my cardiologist weaned me from several of the drugs I'd been taking. The combination of frequent exercise and diminished chemical side effects rejuvenated my cardiovascular system, and during the last few weeks of rehab my cock responded whenever Trevor touched me or I had impure thoughts about him. Twice during the last week of rehab I awoke in the middle of the night while dreaming about my physical therapist, surprised when I attempted to roll over and found my progress impeded by an erection as firm as any I'd had presurgery.

"Ready for graduation?" Trevor asked when I finished my last scheduled workout. By then I had—at least once during the previous weeks—lifted, pulled, pushed, pressed, squeezed, spun or walked on every piece of exercise equipment in the rehabilitation center gym. At home I had moved up from two-pound free weights to fifteen-pound free weights, and I had returned to work with no restrictions on my activities.

Trevor led me into the same private room we'd used when I had shuffled in for my first day of rehab. After I sat on the stool, he had me remove my shirt and again he measured everything. Three inches had disappeared from my waist and my biceps were three-quarters of an inch bigger around. I hadn't believed it was possible, but I was in better shape than when I had arrived. Even my chest hair had regrown, obscuring the ten-inch scar bisecting my chest.

"You've made a lot of progress," Trevor said. He sat on a stool several inches shorter than mine, facing me with his left hand resting on my leg, just above my knee. "It's amazing what you can do now that you couldn't do when you first shuffled in here."

"You wouldn't believe what I'm capable of now." I stared straight into his pale-blue eyes as I reached out and placed my hand on top of his.

He glanced down at our hands but didn't pull his away. When his gaze again met mine, he asked, "Are you healthy enough for private therapy sessions?"

"My doctor seems to think so."

"You realize your insurance doesn't cover private therapy."

I smiled. "What are you suggesting?"

The vertical scar indicating where the surgeon had entered my chest was no longer the angry red welt it had been, but it was still sensitive to the touch. Trevor pressed the tip of his index finger to the top of the scar and traced its length down between the wires still attached to the electrodes stuck to my chest, causing me to shiver. No one had ever touched my scar like that and it was a more intimate act than any other he could have done. My cock reacted immediately, tightening my pants.

"You're not my patient anymore," he said.

"What does that mean?"

"It means I can do this." He leaned forward and lightly pressed his lips against mine. After he drew back, he searched for any sign that I might have been offended or taken aback by his action. When he saw none, he continued. "You can't stop exercising just because it's no longer covered by your insurance. You'll need to join a gym or find some other way to continue the work we've done here."

"But who will ensure that I'm on the right track?"

"I can continue to do that for you," he said. He lowered his voice and leaned forward. "I even know a few exercises we can do in private."

"You'd be willing to do that?"

His left hand slid up my thigh until it stopped less than an inch from my rapidly swelling cock.

I glanced at the door. "Someone might interrupt us."

"Don't worry," he said. "The door's locked."

Trevor undid my belt buckle, unbuttoned my jeans and slid my zipper down. I lifted my buttocks so he could slide my pants down, and when he did the transmitter still hanging from my belt clunked against the stool. I barely noticed the sound and didn't think about it as Trevor reached inside my boxers and wrapped his hand around the base of my cock, capturing some of my untamed pubic hair in his fist.

"I'm surprised it's so hard," I said. "I haven't been exercising it recently."

"Well, it seems to be up for a little physical therapy." Trevor watched my eyes as he stroked upward until his encircling thumb and forefinger reached the helmet head of my cock. Then he stroked back to the base.

He repeated the motion several times until a bead of precum glistened atop the tiny slit. Then he leaned forward, took the head of my cock in his mouth and locked his lips around my glans. He licked away the drop of precum and spanked my cockhead with his tongue as he tightened his fist around the shaft and pumped hard and fast.

My heart began to beat hard and I gripped the stool with both hands to keep from scooting off of it as I thrust my hips forward and back in rhythm to the pumping of Trevor's fist. My balls began to tighten and my cock grew even stiffer. I knew I was about to come, and I couldn't have stopped myself even if I had wanted to. I didn't know how thick the walls were or how well the door sealed in sounds, so I bit my bottom lip to keep from crying out.

I came hard, so hard I jerked involuntarily. I might have fallen if there hadn't been a wall only a few inches behind me that kept me from going backward off the stool. The sudden change in my position caused my pants to slip from my thighs, taking the transmitter with them down to my ankles and pulling the trio of electrodes from my chest.

My cock throbbed inside Trevor's mouth as I fired warm cum against the back of his throat. He swallowed and swallowed again, holding my cock in his mouth until he had sucked it dry. Then he drew away, leaned back and looked up at me.

"You," I said, repeating what I had told him the first time he'd put me on the treadmill, "take my breath away."

I slipped from the stool, tucked my semierect cock into my boxers, and put my clothes in order. Trevor took the transmitter from me, grabbed the clipboard with my paperwork and opened the door. Then he walked me to the nurse's station and looked at the report generated by the EKG. He looked up at me. "You didn't break it."

I lowered my voice as I leaned across the desk. "That thing was recording?"

"Until it fell off," he said as he tapped the report. "I'm no doctor, but I think your heart's made a remarkable recovery."

"Not a complete recovery," I said. I told him about the man who had broken my heart almost a year before my surgery.

"No surgery will cure that," he said.

"But continued exercise with the right partner will." I invited him to dinner the following Friday.

Trevor came directly from work, still wearing his blue scrubs. I greeted him with a kiss and led him into the kitchen where I was preparing boneless pork chops with an orange marmalade sauce, had au gratin potatoes in the oven and a spinach salad in the fridge. I handed him a bottle of wine to open and soon we were flirting, sipping wine and watching the pork chops brown.

"Have you found a gym?"

"Not yet," I admitted. "I really haven't looked."

"You should start," he said as he touched my bicep. "You don't want all our hard work to disappear."

I also didn't want lectures from my cardiologist, who had been quite impressed by the amount of progress I had made in such a short time, thanks to the exercise routine Trevor put me through. "I'll start tomorrow," I said. "Tonight, though, you promised to show me a few exercises we can do in private."

He placed his wineglass on the kitchen counter and then captured my face between his hands. He covered my lips with his and kissed me long, deep and hard. I wanted to wrap my arms around Trevor and pull him close, but I held tongs in one hand, my wineglass in the other, and couldn't reach the counter to put them down. That didn't stop my tongue from meeting his and engaging in a fiery dance of desire.

The kiss didn't end until my knees grew rubbery and I felt as weak as I had the first day Trevor put me on a treadmill. He drew back, picked up his wineglass and said, "That's just the warm-up. Wait 'til we get to the stretching exercises."

I wanted to rush through dinner, but I didn't dare. Once I confirmed that the potatoes were done and the chops were perfect, I served dinner in the dining room. As we ate, we talked, laughed, flirted and drank our way through the bottle of wine.

We didn't bother clearing the table when we finished. I took Trevor's hand and led him into the bedroom where I had already turned down the sheets, had a fresh tube of lube on the nightstand, and had been burning a vanilla-scented candle since midafternoon.

We peeled off our clothes, tossing them aside without care. When we were both naked, I took a moment to appreciate Trevor's sculpted body, which was even better than I had imagined it, before I grabbed his ass and pulled him to me. Our cocks collided, shifted, and then my cock pressed his abdomen and his pressed against mine.

I covered his mouth with mine and shoved my tongue between his lips, tasting orange marmalade and wine when our tongues met. He slipped one hand between us, wrapped his fist around my cock and began tugging at it. I didn't want to come too soon, so I pushed his hand away.

Trevor ended our kiss by pulling away and turning his back. He grabbed the lube, twisted off the top and handed the tube to me. As I slathered a good bit of it up and down the length of my cock, Trevor bent over the bed, braced his knees against the mattress and thrust his ass up at me. I squeezed a good dollop of lube into his asscrack and then used my fingers to massage the tight pucker of his asshole. Soon it opened to one lube-slickened finger and I pistoned my finger in and out. When he seemed relaxed, I pulled my finger free and pressed the head of my cock against Trevor's asshole.

I don't know if he was quite ready, but I pressed forward anyhow, driving my slickened cock deep into him as he cried out. I drew back until only my cockhead remained inside him, and then drove forward again.

As I fucked the physical therapist, I held tight to one of his hips and reached around him with my free hand. After I wrapped my lube-slickened fist around his stiff cock, I began pumping up and down the length of his shaft, my hand not quite in rhythm with my hips.

The closer I came to orgasm, the faster I pumped into Trevor's ass and the faster my hand stroked his cock. He came first, firing a glob of cum onto the sheets and covering my fist with his sexual effluent.

I released my grip on his cock even though he was still coming, and grabbed his other hip. I slammed into him another dozen times, each thrust harder and faster than the one before it.

And then I came.

I came hard, emptying my balls inside his ass as I pressed myself tight against him. My heart beat wildly inside my chest and for a moment I worried that I had overexerted myself. Even as I thought that, I knew that I didn't care.

When I caught my breath and my cock finally stopped spasming in Trevor's ass, I pulled away and flopped onto the bed, barely missing the wet spot he'd created. He climbed into bed beside me.

"Think that would have broken the EKG?" I asked.

"I'm sure of it," he said, out of breath. "It almost broke me."

Trevor spent the night, and the next morning we fucked again. I expected him to leave after I prepared breakfast and we cleaned the dishes from the night before, but he had another idea.

"You're not going to find a gym if I leave you to your own devices," he said, "so get dressed and come with me."

I did as instructed and soon we were walking into a gym not far from the cardiopulmonary rehabilitation center, one where the men at the workout machines were serious about their workouts. The place smelled of sweat and testosterone and the men were dressed in sweats and sleeveless T-shirts. The only music came from the clanking of weights and the grunting of men lifting.

At Trevor's insistence, I joined the gym that day, and when we aren't working out together in my bedroom, we're working out together at the gym he made me join.

I'm now more buff than I've ever been, I've rebuffed the advances of several of the gym's other members and my cardiologist gets happier each time I have a checkup.

Surgery may have repaired my damaged heart, but my physical therapist repaired my broken heart.

# JOCKSTRAPS

## Oleander Plume

I was a freshman in college when my addiction started.

Despite the fact that I loathed the game, I signed up to be equipment manager for the football team just to be near those heavenly boys. Tall and husky, with bulging muscles that stirred a hunger deep inside my balls. I loved watching them interact in the locker room after a game. Hard bodies drenched with sweat, emitting musk like wild beasts about to rut. They never noticed me hulking in the shadows, lost in wild fantasies. Being unseen had its advantages. I could ogle them in plain sight while they stood under the shower spray, naked and glorious, while the steam curled their hair. Each player was enticing in his own way, but one consumed my thoughts more than the others, a brooding hunk named Tyler Monroe.

In my eyes, Tyler was the finest male specimen that ever drew breath. Hairy all over, even his knuckles, like a sexy caveman. His piercing eyes never looked my way, and why would they? I was small framed and androgynous, he was masculine perfection. That sexy boy was the star of my fantasies; they played out like X-rated movies in my head. Tyler sprawled across the bench in the locker room while I worshipped his perfect body with my tongue. Tyler snaking one of those hairy fingers up my ass while I was bent over his lap and squirming against his thighs. I never expected any of my scenarios to come true, until one of them actually did.

It was a Tuesday afternoon. All the players had showered and left for the day, except Tyler. I was folding towels and stealing glances at him while he lathered up his delicious low-hangers. The boy had the most amazing testicles, big and meaty, packed into a baggy sac that almost reached mid-thigh. I wanted to rub my face on that sac, then bury my nose in his dense thatch of pubic hair.

"You like looking at my junk, fag?"

"No, I was checking to see if you were almost finished. I have clean towels."

He shot a glare my way that made me skulk away in fear. Later, in the deserted locker room, he grabbed me from behind and shoved me into a corner.

"I've got a present for you, gay boy."

One heavy arm pinned me in place while his free hand pressed a wad of fabric over my nose. The heavy scent of sweat permeated my senses as I breathed through his jockstrap, the same one that had cradled his perfect scrotum only moments before.

"Open your mouth, taste my jock." I shook my head but he wouldn't let go. His body was pressed so tightly against mine; I could feel his bulge digging into my left buttcheek. "Open up."

I did. The cotton blend was soft against my tongue and I could almost taste him. My dick twitched inside my shorts, and my mind was full of conflicting emotions. It felt strange to be so terrified, yet so turned on.

"Like that? Bet you wish my dick was in your mouth, instead."

His hot breath brushed my ear, sending chills of lust all over my body. He grunted, then started dry-humping me. I turned slightly, so that the hard knot in his pants was hitting my asscrack dead center. Fuck, I wanted him inside. My tongue licked faster and I began to whimper.

"Yeah, eat that jock."

*Bump, bump, bump.* My dick crept out of the waistband of my shorts.

"Tastes good, doesn't it?"

*Bump, bump, bump.* Two hairy digits shoved the jock deeper into my mouth. I opened wider, sucking fingers and cloth while my cock grew even harder. My balls were vibrating, actually vibrating.

"You fucker, you stupid little fucker."

*Bump, bump, bump.* He took his hand from my mouth, but I kept chewing on his jock. His fingers squeezed my hips while he pounded his dick against me.

"Fucker, little fucker."

*Bump, bump, bump.* To my complete and utter shock, he reached inside my shorts and found my sac. His fingers were gentle as they rolled my balls against each other in time with the motion of his pelvis. My whimpering changed to moaning when that same hand moved higher and those hairy fingers wrapped around my dick. Two strokes and my balls emptied. My body went rigid and my calves tightened as my heels rose off the floor.

"Stupid little fucker."

*Bump, bump, bump.* My legs went weak and I could barely stand, but I managed to keep upright while my semen dripped down his hand. He stopped bumping and ground against me instead, faster and faster, until I felt wetness on the small of my back where my shirt had ridden up.

"You made me come, little fucker."

He kissed my neck while I cried like a baby.

"Shh, don't cry. I won't tell, I won't tell anyone."

Tyler thought I was upset, when in actuality, I was the happiest little fucker in the universe and crying out of sheer euphoria. I let him think what he wanted, because I enjoyed the way he was trying to comfort me. He held me close while he tucked my spent dick back inside my shorts, wet tongue on the base of my neck leaving a trail of his guilt on my skin.

"You okay?"

I nodded, his jock still clamped between my teeth. He tried to take it back, but I bit down harder. He smirked and patted my cheek.

"Like that, huh? Want to keep it?"

"Uh-huh."

Tyler smiled a genuine smile. His face was inches from mine, and I thought he was going to kiss me, but his expression changed, going from blissful to somber in a blink.

"This never happened."

He shook his head, then gave me one last brooding glare before leaving me alone in the locker room. I wiped the semen off my back with his jock, then wrapped it in a towel and buried it in the bottom of my backpack before heading home. Once I was in the safety of my single dorm, I stripped naked and played with my dick while I replayed the scene over and over. When I inhaled, I could still smell him, as if the scent of his sweat had been tattooed inside my nostrils. The more I drew in his essence, the more I fell in love, not just with Tyler, but with what was to become my greatest addiction.

Jockstraps. I love the way they cradle a man's balls so lovingly while leaving his ass bare and open. I love the way they smell after an arduous workout. I love the way they feel when I wear them under my clothes. Buying them online from specialty catalogs is my favorite hobby, but the ones I find accidentally intrigue me the most. Two years ago, I took a management

position at a fitness center. One day while inspecting the men's
locker room, I found a jock that had been left behind. There it
was, a tangled wad of fabric peeking out from under a bench,
like a treasure for me to find. In the following months I found
more; it's amazing how many men forget them. I have amassed
quite a hoard that I keep stored in plastic bags to preserve the
scent. Each man has his own unique odor, meant to be savored.
One in particular is my prized possession. Tyler's jock. Even
after six years, his redolence lingers.

My collection plays a part in my complex nightly ritual. First,
I shower. While still damp, I pick a favorite and remove it from
the plastic bag. After inhaling the scent for a while, I rub the
pouch all over my skin, targeting my nipples and cock. Once I'm
hard, the fabric is balled up and shoved into my greedy mouth. I
stand with my face crammed into a corner, then furiously stroke
myself to orgasm. Once a week, I change my routine. Saturday
nights is reserved for Tyler, and I chew on his jock while I fuck
myself with a large dildo, facedown on my bed. The red latex
phallus was chosen specifically because the thick crown reminds
me of Tyler's cock. I pretend he's the one fucking me, owning
me, using me for his pleasure.

Sometimes I cry afterward, I don't know why. Maybe it's out
of loneliness, or maybe it's something else, something deeper
that I don't want to discover. I long to have a boyfriend, but
I'm not out and meeting new people is hard for someone who
is socially awkward. Once, I tried visiting a glory hole, but ran
away in terror when I caught a glimpse of the rough clientele.
So I live alone, and masturbate, that's my life. Until last week,
when a new client joined the health club.

Tyler Monroe.

He still looked amazing. Toned body, like a hairy god. I
watched him shower, staring in rapture as he turned those low-
hangers frothy with soap.

"Billy Lewis. Still like perving on guys in the shower, huh?"

I shrugged, and tried to tear my eyes away from his cock, but I couldn't. "It's really great to see you, Tyler."

He stroked his cock with a soapy hand. "You work here, huh? Thought you were going to be an engineer or something."

My tongue poked my bottom lip, and I struggled to look him in the eyes. "I like working here, it's peaceful."

"Peaceful? Isn't the pay crappy?" He reached between his legs and soaped up his asscrack, all the while staring at me. My balls started vibrating.

"I have a management position, so no, it's really not."

Tyler grunted. "Good for you." He smirked. "Little fucker."

I opened my mouth to utter some random nonsense, but was interrupted when another patron requested clean towels. Later, I ventured back to check the showers, but he was gone. Disappointment jabbed me in the gut until I heard bare feet slapping on the tile behind me.

"Where can we be alone?" Tyler's voice whispered in my ear, deep and throaty, his towel-clad body inches from mine, stirring up memories and longing.

"Follow me," I whispered back.

No one noticed as we slipped inside the storage room. My hands trembled as I locked the door, anticipating what might happen next. I hoped he wanted to give me the deep, hard fucking I craved. His hairy fingers dug into my shoulders when he shoved me against the wall.

"I think about that afternoon all the time, do you?" His eyes were wild, his voice desperate.

"Yeah, sometimes."

He yanked my shirt over my head and tossed it aside. "The rest of the guys thought you looked like a girl, but I thought you were beautiful."

His words rendered me speechless; I could only stand there,

useless, while he undressed me. When he got to my jock, he grinned, then slid it slowly over my hips, kneeling down so he could work the straps over my shoes.

"I've never seen a pink jockstrap before." He raised it to his face and inhaled. "It smells like you." He pressed it into my hand. "Make me eat it."

"What?"

"You heard me, rub it on my face, then make me eat it. Do it." I shyly rubbed my jock over his nose and sexy lips, and he inhaled loudly. "You smell so fucking good."

"I do?"

"Yeah."

He closed his eyes and opened his mouth. Something broke loose inside me, and for the first time in years, I didn't feel like a freak.

"Taste it." Lovingly, so lovingly, I shoved that pink fabric behind his lips. "I'll bet you wish my dick was in your mouth, instead."

Tyler nodded. I rose up on my toes, pushed his head lower and ground my cock against his face. He gripped my ass in both hands and nuzzled my balls. I pulled up my shaft to give him better access.

"Suck me, suck my dick."

He spit out the jock, then used his mouth on my sac, and the warm, wet sensation made my head spin. I rested my back against the wall and watched him work. He spent a lot of time working over my testicles, sucking and licking each one until saliva was dripping down my thighs.

"Tasty little fucker."

"Yeah, keep calling me that. I like when you call me that."

The moment was surreal. Tyler Monroe, on his knees, deep-throating me while he fondled my balls. I watched in amazement as my shaft slid in and out of his mouth; the surface grew wet and glossy, the head practically purple. But it was the sight of those dark eyes staring up at me that put me over the edge.

"That feels so good, I'm not going to last."

I expected him to pull away, but he kept me tight in his mouth and swallowed every drop, then licked the head clean. He smiled at me while my cock throbbed against his cheek.

"You ready to try a bite of mine?"

"No. I want you to fuck me."

He stood up and stared into my eyes. "You sure?"

"Yeah, I want it." I inhaled sharply. "I want your cock in my ass."

"I've wanted to fuck you for so goddamn long."

I couldn't help myself, he was leaning in so close, I had to kiss him. He not only kissed me back, he fucked the inside of my mouth with his tongue. We made out like teenagers, with groping hands, heavy breathing and soft moans. When we finally came up for air, he put the tip of his finger in my mouth, then teased my asshole with it.

"I want you so fucking bad. Are you ready for me?"

My coworker, Lewis, kept condoms and lube in an old Superman lunchbox he kept hidden inside the storage room. I opened it with trembling hands, then handed a foil packet to Tyler. He reached in the box and picked up the bottle.

"We'll need this too. I have a pretty big dick."

"I know." I bent over a stack of cardboard boxes and spread my legs wide. "Put it in quick, don't make me wait."

Tyler stood behind me and kneaded my asscheeks. "I have to get you ready, be patient."

I was so excited; every muscle in my body was taut enough to snap. Tyler poured some lube on his fingers, then rubbed them over my opening.

"I like it already."

"Wait until I get inside, I'm going to fuck you so good."

Just like in my fantasy, one of Tyler's thick fingers worked its way up my ass, gently, slowly. I clenched up at first, but relaxed as he slowly massaged.

"Feels good, doesn't it? Can I try two?"

"I'm ready for your dick."

"Shh, not yet." I felt a second finger stretch its way inside. "That's a good little fucker; open that sweet ass for me."

He whispered in my ear, causing my body to shiver. His lips kissed everywhere, my neck, my shoulder, then slowly down my back until his tongue was dancing over the top of my crack. I winced as he pulled his fingers out, then moaned as he spread me open and massaged my throbbing hole with his tongue.

"Oh, holy hell."

I laid my cheek against the carton I was leaning on; the cardboard under my mouth became damp as my tongue licked in rhythm with Tyler's. While he lapped at my hole, he used his fingers to massage my taint and balls. I was balanced on the tips of my sneakers, leg muscles burning as I opened them wider to his exploring mouth and fingers. Waves of pleasure rippled up my spine, and I had to bite my thumb to keep from crying out.

"I hope you're ready, I don't think I can wait anymore."

"Fuck me."

The words came out as more of a growl. Tyler rubbed the head of his sheathed cock up and down my crack. "You want my dick?"

"Yes, fuck me."

He pushed the tip against my opening, then stopped. "You want my big fat cock up your tight little hole?"

"Shut up and fuck me already!"

Tyler chuckled. "I just don't want to hurt you, that's all."

"Is that why you're being such a tease? I'm not scared, put your dick in me."

"Okay little fucker, you asked for it." His tone didn't match his words, his voice soft and almost pleading. "Here it comes."

The intrusion was softer than I expected, more yielding than my vibrator, and definitely warmer. There was a slight sting at first that disappeared the deeper he penetrated. Once he was halfway inside, he exhaled slowly, then rested his head against my shoulder. His tongue licked, his fingers stroked and I was lost in a thousand dizzying sensations.

"It's so tight, do you like it?"

"Fuck yeah."

"I like it too; damn, you're beautiful." He pulled the elastic band out of my ponytail and wrapped my hair in his fingers. "Pretty little fucker."

My heart was throbbing even more than my anus. His sweet words were like magic and I felt myself open up, allowing his full length to slide inside. He began to thrust, tiny movements that caused my cock to harden again.

"That's my good little fucker, swallow me."

"Fuck me, Tyler, harder."

"I'm going to make you come again." He fisted my dick, and stroked firmly while he fucked me, the sound of skin slapping on skin filling the cramped space. "Can I pound you?"

"Yeah, do it. Fuck me raw."

*Bump, bump, bump.* Tyler grabbed my hips and pistoned wildly.

"Little fucker, you feel so good."

*Bump, bump, bump.* My balls felt swollen, and a heat rose up from my lower belly. A slight twinge of discomfort disappeared when he kissed my neck.

"Sweet little fucker, you're making me come."

"Don't you dare, keep fucking me, don't stop. Don't you fucking stop."

*Bump, bump, bump.* I didn't want any of it to end. Not the blissful sensation of hot friction, not the warmth of his furry chest against my back, not the heavy, plugged-up feeling of his cock inside my ass. I wanted to stay trapped in that moment forever.

"Little fucker, I can't—"

"Yes you can, fuck the cum out of me, do it." He pulled out completely. "What the hell?"

"Shh, I'm going to fuck you so good, tell me when I hit your sweet spot." He plunged back inside, pushing inch by inch until he hit a place that made me whine. "There?"

"Fuck yeah." He targeted that small area, rubbing it with the bulbous crown until I almost passed out from sexual euphoria. "Fuck, oh fuck, so good. Uhn. Uhn. Uhn."

This was followed by a stream of curse words that were forced from my throat while his cock worked over my prostate gland. He didn't just fuck me, he sent me to heaven and before I could try to catch my breath, I was spewing semen everywhere.

"Can I come now, little fucker?"

I groaned a response and the bumping stopped. His dick seemed to get larger inside me, then he buried his face in my hair and growled as he came. When he was finished, he stroked my hips and tried to catch his breath.

"Don't move, stay inside me."

"I can't move, you have a death grip on my dick." He tried to pull out but I clenched harder.

"No, stay."

Tyler rubbed my nipples and nuzzled my ear. "That was the tightest ass I've ever fucked."

"Was I okay?"

"You were more than okay."

His dick was still twitching inside me when a knock on the storage room door brought me back to reality.

"Yeah?"

"Billy, are you in there? I need some paper towels for the men's room."

It was Lewis. My eyes glanced to the Superman lunchbox and I stifled a laugh. "Um, just taking inventory in here, I'll bring some with me when I come out."

Tyler slowly withdrew, then yanked off the condom and tossed it in a trash can while I cleaned up the puddle I'd left on the floor. "Do you think he knew what we were doing in here?"

"I'm sure. He brings his boyfriend back here all the time."

Tyler wrapped his towel around his hips. "Can you hear them fucking?"

"Not really." I pulled my polo shirt over my head, then smiled. "But then again, I try really hard not to."

"Why?"

"I suppose because I'm slightly jealous."

I worked my shorts over my sneakers and pulled them up. Tyler picked up my jock from the floor, smiled, then stuffed it into his mouth. I laughed and tried to snatch it back, but he wouldn't let go.

"Like that, huh? Want to keep it?"

He nodded.

# STEEL DREAMS

## Logan Zachary

A nd to my son, Thomas Michael Weldon, I bequeath my
business, Steel Dreams." The lawyer looked over his
glasses and stared straight at me.

I looked around the small office. Mom wore her designer
little black dress. Max Allen wore a flannel shirt and ripped
jeans, and Penny May filled her sleek black pants suit. They all
glared at me.

What was the problem?

Dad had given me the gym, a small gym. That's all. Why
did they want that? Dad always loved when I came down to the
gym. Max Allen didn't like it. He had his booze and babes to
deal with.

Dad's will didn't say anything about a dollar amount for me.
His will gave money to my brother and my sister, while Mom
kept the house and the rest of his money.

"Who wants that sweaty, stinky old gym anyway," Mom
said. She rubbed Max Allen and Penny May's backs.

I stood up, walked out and didn't look back.

* * *

I parked my car and walked across the lot to the front door of Steel Dreams. I didn't have the keys yet, so I used the front door. With all of Dad's businesses, he never allowed any family member to have a key to Steel Dreams. I pulled the heavy glass door open, and Jimmy, the front desk guy, smiled as he saw me.

"Thomas, what are you doing here?" he asked. Jimmy Bond had been a three-time bodybuilder world champion, and his body had appeared on many sporting goods ads, equipment and even breakfast cereal. He was a deep brown African American, and his shirt hugged his body like a second skin. His waist was narrow and his thighs bulged, as did his booty.

I could see the outline of his meaty cock inside the sweat-pants. Unlike most bodybuilders, he was hung and had trouble covering his junk in a Speedo, especially at competitions. I tried to avoid looking down at his groin, but I couldn't help myself, and my own dick rose in my pants. I had seen Jimmy in the shower many times. I had jacked off to him many times. His huge uncut dick amazed me, and I had only seen it soft.

Jimmy came around the front desk and pulled me into his arms. He hugged me close, smothering my face against his massive chest. I tried to hug him back, but my arms didn't reach all the way around. I inhaled as he held me. Old Spice, manly sweat and Irish Spring soap rose from his warm embrace. I sunk into him and tried to keep my erection from touching him.

Jimmy finally released me and held me at arm's length. "I'm so sorry about your dad. He was a good man."

A tear formed in my eye and threatened to roll down my face. I blinked hard and squinted my eyes shut. "I came to...I guess, well, Dad gave the gym to me..." my voice trailed off.

Jimmy nodded slowly. "His office hasn't been touched since he…"

"I know, Jimmy. I'm not looking at changing anything, so your job is safe. Don't worry about that."

"I wasn't worried about that." He rubbed my shoulder. "I'm here if you need me."

"Thanks."

"His office is unlocked. I lock it every night before I go home and unlock it when I get here. That's how he wanted it, and"— he paused for a long second—"I'm still doing it." He motioned to the door on his left.

"No problem," I said, and forced a smile as I wiped at my eye. The tear rolled over my finger, and I felt something roll down my throat.

"So you inherited the gym. He never told me what his plans were with his businesses. I'm glad it was you he gave it to, because your brother and mother would sell it so fast." He closed his mouth and bit his lower lip, as if he had said too much. "Just call if you need anything."

"I know my family all too well." I smiled. "I'll call if I need anything." I walked to my dad's office door and slowly turned the knob. How many times had his hand touched that door? I pushed the door open and flipped on the light. As I turned to close the door, Jimmy waved at me.

As soon as the door closed I inhaled deeply, drawing in the smell of Dad: VO5 hair oil and peppermint Life Savers: Dad. I sat at his desk and looked at the half roll of peppermint Life Savers. I guess they didn't work. I remembered buying him the fancy variety pack as a kid at Christmas time, and he always gave me most of the rolls, except for the peppermint ones.

I sat in his chair and let the warm leather cradle me. I closed my eyes and let memories flood over me.

* * *

A knock on the door startled me out of my daydreams.

"Is everything okay, boss?" Jimmy asked, concern filling his voice.

I looked at the clock. How long had I been out? It was after one o'clock. I rose on unsteady legs and opened the door. I forced a smile. "I'm fine. Sorry to scare you."

"Did you want anything to eat? I was going to run out for lunch."

My stomach was empty. "I don't want you going out of your way to pick up something for me."

"I can stop anywhere you want."

"All I want is a turkey sandwich and a Coke."

"Done. No one should need me, so you don't have to man the front desk if you don't want. Maybe you would like to take a tour of the gym and see how things have changed. Your dad upgraded a lot of things."

I nodded. "I'll do that."

Jimmy headed out the door.

I looked through the window into the weight room, and the machines and weights shined in the light. I walked down the hallway and entered the remodeled locker room. A soft cushioned mat covered the floor and wooden lockers lined the walls. A huge hot tub bubbled, and a huge glass room filled with steam and smelling of eucalyptus dominated one corner. As I neared, I heard moans coming from inside, and low masculine groans.

A naked, muscular ass pressed against the glass and disappeared. A bearded face appeared and disappeared with each grunt. The speed increased as did the volume of the grunts.

Skin slapped against skin as the moans deepened. A tongue licked the window, and then suddenly a naked, hairy man's body was visible. His huge, hard cock was pressed against the glass and suddenly exploded. A thick blob of come splattered over the glass. The white load slowly dripped down as another blast hit. Two more orgasms shot out of the huge dick and slid slowly down.

The man remained pinned against the glass and slowly dropped to his knees. His tongue licked the cream from the glass wall and spread it out farther.

A loud slap echoed through the locker room. "Thanks, man, that was hot. Let's hit the showers." The steam room door started to open, and I panicked.

I jumped back, and my feet slipped on the wet tiled floor. My back hit the full-length mirror behind me, and the whole wall opened up. I fell backward and into the wall. I landed on the foam mat that covered the floor as the mirror swung back into place.

As I looked over my shoulder, I realized the whole wall and all the mirrored walls were two-way mirrors. I rose to my feet and followed the tightest ass ever into the shower room. A trail of semen ran down the inside of his thighs starting from his glutes. The other man exited the steam room, his huge cock and low-hanging balls swinging between his legs and dripping with come.

As I moved over to get a better view, I saw a small camera aimed into the shower room. The red light blinked as it recorded the two men.

The showers started, and the hot water cascaded over the oily bodybuilders' torsos. The streaks of semen washed along their bodies and swirled down the drain.

My cock swelled in my pants, and I adjusted myself as it grew.

The bald man soaped up the man with a buzz cut. His hands rubbed between the other man's cheeks, and his finger entered his butt as he cleaned up his tight, pink opening.

The buzz-cut guy moaned, just as he had in the steam room.

Thick creamy come poured out of his bottom and washed away.

Baldy foamed him up and washed every inch of his body. His own cock grew in the shower and rubbed along his body like a loofa.

"Thomas?" Jimmy called.

I startled and raced for the swinging mirror. I pushed through the mirror, slipped it back into place, and bolted down the rows of lockers. I bounced off Jimmy's chest at the locker room entrance.

"Whoa. Are you okay? You're all flushed." Jimmy held up a small bag.

"Just...remembering and exploring," I said, breathlessly.

Jimmy eyed me suspiciously.

"Mom and Max Allen hated this place. They never understood why Dad or I loved this placed so much. Mom always said this place never made any money, and she hated the long hours Dad put into this failing business, or so she said. With all that, I don't know why they are so mad at me for inheriting it."

Jimmy handed me my lunch. "We need to talk about the business. There are a few things you need to know, but that can wait. Go eat and we'll talk later. I have a client's special session coming up." He turned and headed back to his station.

I went to Dad's office and quickly ate my sandwich. Between bites of turkey, I rifled through Dad's hard drive.

Nothing.

Then I remembered the something: I slipped out of the office and entered the security room. The space was lined with shelves of DVDs. There was a computer on, and I could see the entire gym in various camera views on the screen.

A handsome man entered the gym and headed toward Jimmy's desk. In another camera view, Jimmy stood and extended his hand in welcome.

Jimmy greeted the handsome man and took him into the

gym, and I watched him enter a private exercise room. I knew he took on several private clients and helped them with their stage presentation and bodybuilding.

I left the security room and raced to the locker room.

"Head into the private room and I'll be right there." Jimmy waved the man on and walked to the sink and washed his hands. As he reached for a paper towel, he turned his back to me.

I looked around the locker room and saw no one was looking, so I slipped into the mirror and made my way through the maze of walls. It took me a few minutes to find the private room Jimmy was using. I gasped as I saw the handsome man.

Jimmy had him bound and gagged. He hung from his wrists suspended from the ceiling and his naked body swung free. His balls were tied tight with a leather strap and his penis stood straight out.

Jimmy wrapped his hands with tape and started to give his torso a few jabs.

The man's muscles tightened and relaxed. He spun around and his amazing ass flashed me.

Jimmy punched his butt and a red fist appeared on his pale white bottom.

The naked man's trunk elongated and tightened, making his muscles pop out and show in fine detail.

Jimmy did the boxing dribble to his long, hanging pair.

The man's smoothly shaved orbs bounced in his long scrotal sac. His penis jumped and down as his balls were knocked around. A few thick drops flew in all directions.

"We need to toughen you up." Jimmy punched him a few more times and spun his body.

The smooth balls rose up.

Jimmy stroked his thick penis, as he pulled his hand to the tip. A gush of precome flowed over his palm. "You are too easily excited and lose your focus. You can't be sprouting an erection in your Speedos. You are too big to be held in the tiny fabric."

The red light on the camera blinked as it recorded. I wondered what happened to all the recordings.

Jimmy opened a cabinet in the room and pulled out a Crisco container.

As the naked man saw this, he pulled and twisted against his restraints.

Jimmy donned a long black rubber glove and reached into the can and pulled out a handful of grease. He untied the man's legs as he swung and with his gloved hand, he sought out his hairy opening between his beautiful buttocks. He smeared it all around the hole and slipped a finger inside. He wiggled it back and forth before pulling it out and inserting two into him.

The man's whole body tensed and the muscles stood out in his neck.

"Relax, you've done this before. It hurts more when you fight it." Jimmy pulled his two fingers out and brought all his fingertips together into a cone. He pressed against the hole and pressed.

The man spread his legs.

Jimmy grabbed his cock with the other hand and started to jack him off, long, slow strokes that pulled his balls up. His hand entered a little more. He jerked him off faster as he felt the man relax, and then he thrust his hand inside.

The man screamed into his gag.

Jimmy soothed his body by gently rocking back and forth as he caressed his dick. Back and forth he jacked the thick cock and inserted his hand deeper into his ass.

Sweat broke out over the naked man's body and rolled down onto the rubber mat on the floor. A small pool formed under his dangling feet.

Jimmy increased his speed and his depth.

Trails of sweat rolled down the naked man's bruised body.

He swung his body in rhythm with Jimmy's assault.

I reached down and rubbed my dick as I watched.

Jimmy worked faster and faster as his hand ventured deeper, past the wrist and midway up his forearm.

The naked man screamed as his cock exploded in Jimmy's hand; wave after wave of come flowed out of the thick cock and splattered on the mat in the pool of sweat.

Jimmy went on as the protests got louder and louder and the hanging man begged him to stop.

Another explosion of come shot out of his cock and sprayed across Jimmy's shirt.

Jimmy smiled as he slowed, but kept jacking. He pulled his hand out of the man's ass and held his hole wide open at the widest part of his hand. Melted Crisco plopped into the pool of semen and sweat.

Jimmy removed his hand and finally let the man alone.

He snorted out a big gust of air and let his body go loose, hanging limp from the ceiling.

Jimmy wiped his hand clean with a paper towel before washing both hands in the sink.

I moaned as I got close to coming.

Jimmy must have heard me and stopped washing.

I covered my mouth and slowly backed out of the viewing room. I hurried to the locker room and made sure the coast was clear before racing back to my dad's office.

At nine, I locked the front door and headed back toward dad's office—I mean, my office.

"Anything else, Thomas?" Jimmy rose to his feet and stepped into my path.

"Is there a problem?" I asked. My eyes scanned his face and slowly worked down his body. Did he know I had found the secret room? Did he know I had watched him...? I swallowed hard, and then my gaze dropped lower, and I saw a huge bulge in his sweats.

"Thomas, we need to talk." His hand reached out and touched my shoulder.

I looked into his brown eyes. I could feel my pupils dilate, and I could see his doing the same. This wasn't happening.

His hand slid up my neck and his hand cupped my ear. He massaged my earlobe. His hand pulled my head closer to his.

I could feel his breath on my face. I licked my lips as his mouth drew closer. "Jimmy, I…"

His mouth came down on mine and pressed lightly against it. I opened my mouth, and my tongue entered his.

His tongue tasted mine, and they tangled together. He pushed in deeper, and I opened wider.

My hands slipped down his shirt and ventured underneath. The hair crackled with static electricity as my fingers combed through it. I felt for his nipples and found them erect. I pinched and twisted them harder and harder.

His hands grabbed my ass and kneaded my glutes.

I pressed my pelvis against his and ground my erection against his. Heat radiated from our groins as the embrace tightened. My hands headed south and pushed his sweats down over his hairy ass. Digging deeper and deeper into his muscles, the hair tickled my cock as I got closer to his tight hole. My tip brushed his pink pucker and circled it, testing it, teasing it.

His sphincter pulsated under my touch.

I pressed harder and felt it release. I entered him slightly. I moved closer to him, and he backed up.

His back hit the office door, and we entered dad's office. Jimmy's body hit his desk and lay across it.

I climbed on top of him and straddled his torso.

He moaned into my mouth.

I broke our kiss and licked down his stubble-covered neck

as I pushed his shirt up over his chest. My mouth came down on his nipple and I nibbled on it, then rolled the nub with my tongue as I bit down a little harder.

Jimmy's hands guided my head and held it on his nipple.

My hands reached down and pushed the waistband down in front of his pants.

His huge uncut penis swung free and slapped his belly. A wet spot appeared where the precome splattered out of his foreskin as it hit his treasure trail.

I grasped his girth in my palm and rubbed gently up and down. His foreskin pulled back, and precome flowed out and ran along his thick shaft.

He threw his head back and thrust his hips into my hand. His hands worked on my pants and pulled them down my hips.

My cock escaped my pants and rubbed along his.

I kicked off my shoes and stepped out of my pants.

"I've waited so long for this," Jimmy said. He lifted his legs for me to remove his sweats. Once his hairy legs were loose, he arched his back and raised them up. His pink pucker came into view. His glutes tensed and made his butt wink at me. He reached over his head and pulled open a desk drawer. When he brought his arm down, a small bottle of lube was offered to me.

I didn't hesitate. I oiled up my cock and his hole.

"Hurry," he begged.

My fingers entered him and lubed his tube. I guided my dick along his hairy crease and it slid easily. I teased the opening by circling it with the fat mushroom head of my dick. I stepped closer and pressed against him.

He relaxed and started to swallow me. He winced as the head spread him to his maximum and stretched him wider. He bore down on me, and I popped inside. He wrapped his long legs around me and pulled me all the way in.

I gasped from the sensation. As my balls hit his butt, I almost shot my load. I held perfectly still so not to stimulate another nerve and thought *Baseball, baseball, baseball.*

Jimmy loosened and tightened his legs and started to make my body rock back and forth.

I closed my eyes and prayed, *Let me last, let me last.* I grabbed his cock and stroked it. His balls rose up as I plunged forward. He was so tight and warm, waves of pleasure flowed over my body. I quickened my pace as the joy intensified.

Jimmy thrust his penis into my fist as he felt me slam into his ass. He bore down on my dick, tightening his muscles to add more sensation over my cock.

Sweat dripped down my face and burned my eyes. I bit my lower lip as I thrust deeper. The pleasure grew and grew, I couldn't stop it. I wanted more. With each thrust into him, my balls slapped his ass and bounced off.

Jimmy spread his legs wider and let his head fall back off the edge of the desk. His cock exploded in my hand, a hot, thick white cream spurting across his chest and glistening on his sweaty torso. More semen flowed out of his foreskin and ran over my hand.

As the next wave flowed over my fingers, my dick shot a load into him. I plunged in again, deeper, and held myself buried inside. My cock milked another orgasm from his dick. I massaged his come into his hair.

His skin rippled under my touch. I held still, deep in his bowels, but his ass sucked on my tender cock and forced another spasm out. I couldn't take the sensation anymore. I pulled out of him with a loud pop. The removal overstimulated my dick, and I collapsed on top of him. Our bodies slid against and along each other as our semen and sweat mixed together. My cock's shaft ran alongside his, and we both shuddered, unable to move as we tried to catch our breath.

I eventually rolled off and lay next to him, looking at the ceiling, come and sweat dripping onto the desk.

Jimmy rolled onto his elbow and kissed me. "I have wanted to do that forever, but…"

"I know. I've wanted that too, but I didn't know you…"

His finger touched my lips.

Then the thought flashed through my mind. Did Dad know?

Jimmy smiled down at me. "He loved you dearly. He knew all about you, but felt you didn't want to talk about it, so he never asked."

"Was he…?"

Jimmy smiled and shook his head. "I don't kiss and tell. What happens between two people should stay between them. No need to brag or disclose secrets and such."

"Was he happy?"

"This was his home. The men loved him, and he loved them. This wasn't work, this was his life. He died here, and he died happy."

"No wonder the rest of the family hates me and this place." I felt a wad of goo flow along my hip and tickle the nerves, making me shiver.

"Are you cold?" Jimmy pulled me closer to warm me up.

"I'm fine, just dripping."

"We should hit the showers." His smile told me he wanted to wash up and then more. He scooted to the edge of the desk and stood. His cock, still semierect and leaking from his foreskin, bobbed in front of me. He extended his hand to help me up.

I rose and watched as rivulets ran down his body and pooled on the office floor. As we walked naked to the shower room, Jimmy took my hand and squeezed it gently.

"I'm moving here and taking over the gym," I said. "You have a job for as long as you want." We stopped, and I looked

into his eyes. I cupped his face and pulled it to mine. I kissed
him deeply, tasting him.

He wrapped his arms around me, pressing his body against
mine. "I have an extra room at my house if you need," Jimmy
said.

"I get my own room?" I asked, somewhat disappointed.

He smiled. "I have a king-size bed and hate to sleep alone.
The other room can be vacant as far as I am concerned." He
squeezed my ass. "Besides, it's my turn now."

"Gotta catch me if you want it," I said as I ran into the
showers, but I slowed on the wet tile. I didn't want to slip and
fall, or so I told myself as his arms wrapped around me.

I looked up at the tiled ceiling and said, "Thanks, Dad."

# THE ARTISTRY
# OF STEAM

Brent Archer

Hey Clara, I'm heading out early. I got the report done for Austin and emailed it to him." Bryan Fleming waved to the dean of education's assistant as he strode out of the University of Washington administration offices. He'd finished classes for the day, and the admin office was dead, so he decided to go down to the gym and get a good workout.

He walked through Red Square and turned down the roadway toward the fountain. *Too hazy today to see Mount Rainier.* Continuing across campus, he noticed several hot young men glancing his way. There were probably women looking too, but he didn't really pay attention.

He smiled at each as he caught his eye. *I can't wait to get to the gym. Nothing like a sweaty college stud to make my workout complete.* Quickening his pace, he arrived at the Intramural Activities Building and flashed his student ID at the young woman at the reception desk. She barely noticed and waved him on, so he proceeded to the locker room.

As he opened the door, the musky scent of sweaty college

boys blasted his senses. He inhaled deeply, and his cock stirred in his slacks. Walking to his usual locker, he surveyed the room of half and fully naked young bucks. *Nice selection today.*

He opened the locker and unbuttoned his white dress shirt. A dark-haired young man opened the locker two down from his. "Hey."

Bryan grinned. "Hey yourself. How's it hanging, Eric?"

"Nice and long. Just how you like it." He dropped his towel, and Bryan took in the young man's body. Eric had a muscular chest dusted with short dark hair. Erect nipples poked out of the stubble, and a trimmed treasure trail led from his eight-pack abs to a long thick cock.

"You know it. It's amazing how you're both a shower and a grower."

A smirk formed across Eric's face. "You'll have to get another taste of it later. I got class until six. Come by my dorm room after that if you want."

Bryan's dick filled out as he thought of sucking Eric's cock. "I'll be there. We can grab a quick dinner and then spend the evening fucking."

Eric gave Bryan's nipple a squeeze, sending a jolt of lust directly to his expanding hardness. "It's a date." He turned to get his clothes out of his locker as Bryan admired his firm ass.

He gave the pert cheeks a slap. "I'll be looking forward to tapping this."

Eric laughed. "We'll see. You haven't managed to get that huge dick of yours inside me yet."

"Just a matter of time and relaxation. I have the time. You just have to relax."

Eric pulled on his clothes as Bryan changed out of his and into shorts and a tank top.

"See you later, Bry." Eric waved and left the locker room.

Watching after him for a moment, Bryan shook his head. *I*

*need to find a guy to top me. All these college guys want is a hard fuck. Guess I'm one of them.*

Bryan closed and locked his locker, and walked to the weight room. He took a couple of small weights from the rack and began his workout. Surveying the room, he locked eyes with an older guy as he changed the weight on the barbell and sat on the bench.

The man smiled and spread his legs wide as he lay back and put his hands to the bar. Bryan willed his cock not to tent his gym shorts. *Holy fuck, what a handsome hunk.* Dark hair, midthirties, with a nice smile, firm chin, muscled pecs barely contained in his T-shirt, and thick muscular legs with dark hair running from his waist to his ankles. From the look of the bulge in his shorts, this guy packed a large set of equipment.

Bryan returned his free weights to the wall-mounted shelves and walked over to the handsome man. "Hi, I'm Bryan. Need a spot?"

"Sure, that'd be great. I'm Todd."

Todd took the bar off the rack and began his routine. Bryan kept his fingers under the bar to be sure it didn't fall. After nineteen reps, Todd's strength faltered, and Bryan grabbed the barbell, keeping it from falling on the exercising man's chest. Together, they settled it back in its resting place and Todd sat up.

"Sorry. I got distracted by what's up your shorts."

Bryan smirked. "If you want a closer look, how about we finish up our workout and head to the showers?"

"Sounds good to me."

They hurried through the remainder of their routines, and then walked to the locker room together. Todd stopped two rows from Bryan's locker.

"This is me. I'll get out of these clothes and meet you under the water."

Bryan nodded. "See you shortly." He hurried to his locker and stripped down. Grabbing his towel, he strutted to the shower stalls. *There's a frisky crowd today. I don't usually see so many randy men here.*

He hung his towel on the hook and entered a stall, leaving the curtain open. Turning on the spray, he stood under the cascading water and looked across to an empty stall. A few moments later, Todd appeared with a towel wrapped around his waist.

*He's even hotter out of his clothes. He's the sexiest guy here by far.* Todd pulled the cloth away and put it on the hook. He nodded to Bryan, stepped into the opposite stall and turned on the water. *Whoa.* Todd's defined abs were shaved clean, and pointed down to a neatly trimmed patch of hair surrounding a thick cock. As Bryan watched, it hardened, and his jaw dropped at the sheer size.

Todd winked as he soaped his body and gave his shaft a few tugs. He turned to face the showerhead, and Bryan stared at his lightly haired firm ass. A thrill of desire rippled through him, and his cock expanded. Todd turned off his shower and grabbed his towel, securing it around his waist as he moved toward the steam room.

Bryan shut off the water and followed him. He opened the door, and steam swirled around him. As his eyes grew accustomed to the dim lighting, he saw Todd sitting naked against the wall on the far side of the room. He sat down next to the dark-haired man.

"Looks like we're all alone."

"Yup."

Bryan removed his towel, and dropped to his knees in front of Todd. "I've got to suck you."

Todd nodded as he spread his legs. "Go for it."

Bryan wrapped his hand around the hard shaft and licked

the head. Taking more of Todd's cock into his mouth, he bobbed his head up and down, swirling his tongue. Todd rewarded him with moans, and put his hands on his head.

Voices outside the door brought Bryan to his feet. *Damn it.* They quickly covered their erections as the door opened and three guys walked in bragging about the girls they planned to bang that night.

Todd stood up and left the room. Bryan followed and caught up with him in the hallway.

"Is there somewhere else we can go to continue?"

Todd grinned. "Sure. I have an art gallery off campus. We could go there. The back room is nice and private, and my staff have the week off."

They rinsed and dried off, and then quickly dressed. Chatting as they strolled to the parking lot, Bryan spied a red Mustang from the sixties. "That's a sweet car. I'd love a ride in it."

Todd pulled out his keys. "Well, get in."

Bryan turned to him. "No way."

"I've had it a couple years. Bought it off an older lady after her husband died. It only had forty thousand miles on it."

"What a score."

Todd chuckled. "We'll get to that."

They climbed into the car, and Todd put it in gear. "I love manual transmissions." The car roared to life and they sped out of the parking lot.

"Are you a student here on campus?" Todd asked as they cruised down Montlake Boulevard.

"Yeah. This is my second year. I hope to study abroad next year."

"Oh, where?"

"England."

Todd nodded. "You'll have a lot of fun there. The guys are hot, the culture's ancient and the tea's an experience."

"I'm looking forward to it."

Todd pulled the Mustang into a parking stall in front of a small building. A sign over the door caught Bryan's attention. *Downing Artistry.* Todd put the key into the lock, opened the door and ran to the back of the shop to turn off the alarm. Bryan eyed the art on the wall. Several modern paintings lined one side of the room, and ten Roman sculptures dominated the back corner.

"Nice place."

Todd opened a door set into the back wall. "Thanks. Here's the office. It's a bit small, but I'm sure we can make it work."

Bryan chuckled. "My, you're eager."

"My cock didn't get soft after you stopped sucking me in the steam room."

Bryan squeezed by him and into the office, quickly stripping out of his clothes. Todd whistled as he shut the door and unzipped his pants. "You're a sexy guy, Bryan. I hope you'll let me fuck that sweet ass of yours." Bryan stood before the older man, and Todd brought his hand to his cheek.

A rush of desire made Bryan whimper. "I want you to ride me hard." He dropped to the floor. "First, though, I want to suck you some more." Opening his mouth, he sucked in Todd's entire erection, closing his eyes as it hit the back of his throat. He bobbed his head back and forth, running his tongue on the bottom of the shaft as he pleasured the older man.

"Oh, shit, you gotta stop or I'll shoot." Todd pushed on Bryan's shoulders.

Bryan sat back, letting the throbbing cock fall from his lips. "I want you to fuck me now."

"Then get on that chair and get ready." Todd pointed to a swivel office chair in front of a small desktop.

As Bryan climbed onto the chair, Todd opened a drawer in the desk. Bryan watched him take a bottle of lube and a condom out. He ripped open the wrapper and rolled it onto his shaft, then squirted a dollop of lube onto his fingers. Bryan groaned as Todd slid one of his digits inside Bryan's tight hole.

"Damn, buddy, this is gonna be a good fuck if you stay this tight."

"I don't bottom often."

"Oh?"

"Most guys take one look at my cock and want me to drill them. Every once in a while it's nice to find a guy willing to top me."

"I'm more than willing." Todd slid another finger in and rotated them.

Bryan moaned as the slight sting turned into an intense warmth, and jumped when Todd stabbed at his prostate. His cock sprang to full hardness.

"Guess you like that. You ready for me?"

"Just go slow at the beginning. Once I'm used to it, you can fuck as hard as you want."

Bryan looked behind him and watched as Todd put lube on his dick. After a couple of tugs, he lined up and slid the head inside Bryan's tight entrance. Bryan gasped at the size and willed his muscles to relax and open up. After a moment, he pushed back against the hard shaft, and more of Todd's erection slid inside him. Once Todd bottomed out, he held still.

The pain gave way as Bryan held on to the back of the chair. "Go for it. Give me that monster."

Todd pulled out almost all the way and slammed back in. "Damn that feels good." He pounded Bryan hard and fast, and then angled to hit his prostate on each thrust.

Bryan's grip on the chair tightened, his balls tingling. *Shit, he's gonna fuck a load out of me.* He threw his head back as his orgasm overtook him. "I'm close."

Todd's rhythm increased. "Wait for me, buddy. I'm almost

there." The chair squeaked and threatened to collapse as it pounded against the desk with each thrust. Todd grabbed Bryan's shoulders and slammed deep into him.

"Oh, fuck," Bryan yelled as his cock blasted the chair with his load. His eyes closed as he rode out the orgasm with Todd buried inside him.

Todd shuddered behind him and thrust a couple more times. "Here it comes." He pulled Bryan back against him and wrapped his arm around Bryan's chest. The older stud roared out his explosion as he filled the condom inside Bryan's ass.

As Todd's softening cock slipped out of him, Bryan got off the chair on wobbly legs and pressed his body against Todd. Bryan liked the feel of Todd's smooth skin against his. He wrapped his arms around the stud.

Todd kissed the top of his head. "Wow. I haven't come like that in a long time. Thank you."

"That was amazing." They held each other for a few moments. The warmth and comfort in their embrace made Bryan sleepy. He yawned and pulled away. "I need to get going."

Todd got a towel from the drawer and wiped off the chair. He fell into it, legs spread and arms at his sides. "I hope I can see you again."

Bryan zipped and buttoned his jeans, conflicted at the swirling emotions the intimate embrace stirred in him. "Sure. Thanks for a great workout."

"See you at the gym."

Bryan grabbed his bag and took one last look at the handsome man sprawled in the swivel chair. Todd's relaxed smile gave Bryan deep satisfaction that he could pleasure such a handsome man. *Yeah, I want to see him again.* He opened the door. "I look forward to it."

* * *

The next day, Bryan could hardly wait to get off work. *I hope I get another round with Todd.* He checked his watch and packed his books into his backpack. *At last.*

"I'm out, Clara. See you tomorrow."

"Where are you off to this evening?"

Bryan slung his pack over his shoulder. "The gym. I'm going for another workout."

"Didn't you work out yesterday?"

"Yeah, but I want to do extra work on my flexibility."

Clara raised an eyebrow but didn't say anything else.

Bryan ran to the IMA Building and flashed his student ID to the bored girl at the desk. Peering into the weight room, his heart sank. No Todd. He continued on to the locker room and stripped quickly out of his clothes. *This is the same time as yesterday. Surely he'll be here.*

He strode to the showers and rinsed off, then hurried to the steam room. A blast of steam met him as he opened the door. Inside, someone sat against the far wall. *There he is.* Bryan closed the door and padded across the wet floor to the opposite bench. *Crap. Not Todd.*

The young man sitting on the tiled bench smiled at him and let his towel slip down his leg. Bryan's cock stirred as he looked over his companion in the steam room. Early twenties, dark hair, blue eyes, a wisp of hair in the middle of a defined chest, and a large, thick cock between thin legs.

"How's it going?"

Bryan nodded as he sat down. "Good." His dick twitched under his towel as he looked over the young man again. "What are you up to?"

"Just looking for a little action. You?"

Bryan pulled his towel away, revealing his plumped up cock. "Same."

"I'm Tony."

"Bryan. You suck?"

In response, Tony knelt before him and opened his mouth. Bryan stroked himself to full hardness and then leaned back against the wall with his arms behind his head. Tony swirled his tongue around the head, and then took the whole thing to the root. Bryan sighed in pleasure as the young man between his legs sucked him.

Pulling off, Tony grabbed his towel and took a condom from beneath it. "I could use a good fucking. You interested?"

With the expert blow job, Bryan didn't need to think twice. "Rubber me up and get ready for a hard ride."

Tony ripped open the package and rolled the condom onto Bryan's shaft. He spat onto the rubber, stood up and turned around, sinking his ass down onto Bryan's cock. Sweat ran down Tony's back as Bryan thrust into him.

"Fuck, you've got a fine ass."

"And you're huge." Tony yelped at a deep thrust, and Bryan brought his hand around to cover his mouth.

"Keep it down. I don't want to get caught." He stood up, his cock still firmly planted inside Tony's ass, and pressed the young man against the wall. He rammed home, and Tony yelled into his hand. Thrusting harder and faster, he felt his buddy shudder and his ass clamp down.

"Coming...AAAAHHHHH!" Tony's muffled cry accompanied a rhythmic massaging of Bryan's cock.

Bryan thrust deep one last time and exploded into the condom, wrapping his arm around Tony and biting down on his shoulder, trying to keep his orgasm quiet. Tony shuddered under him and pressed his head against the tiled wall.

Softening, Bryan's cock slipped from the limp, naked twink. Tony pulled away from Bryan's grip and smiled. "Nice, man. That was fucking hot. I come here Tuesdays, Thursdays and

Saturdays. Hope I see you again."

Bryan sat down on the bench. "Yeah, sure. I'd like that."

Tony grabbed his towel, flashed Bryan the peace sign and exited the steam room. Bryan slipped off the used condom and tied it off. He gathered up the wrapper and left the steam room, throwing away the evidence of his play into a trash can in the shower room.

After washing off, he left the IMA gym and found a coffee shop on University Avenue. He ordered an espresso and sat at a table facing the street. *Maybe Todd will be there tomorrow. It'd be fun to share that hot bottom I met today with him.*

Bryan didn't see Todd in the gym again that quarter, but he had several hot times in the steam room with Tony. He varied the times and days he went to work out, but couldn't seem to find Todd there. Disappointed, he left for his parents' house in Spokane at the end of spring quarter.

After summer break, he signed up for an Art as Life class. The first day of autumn quarter, he walked into the Art Building and took his seat in the back of the classroom. A few minutes later, Todd strode into the class and set the books he carried onto the lectern.

"Good afternoon, class. I'm Professor Downing. I'll be teaching this course since Professor Crawford got overloaded this fall with too many classes. We'll go over the syllabus, and then spend the rest of our time today on our first lecture." He walked to the front row of chairs and handed a sheaf of papers to the students.

Bryan's jaw dropped. *He's a professor?*

Todd looked toward the back of the room. The professor raised an eyebrow and the ghost of a smile lit up his face before he returned to the lectern and started speaking.

After class, Bryan waited until the room emptied. Todd gathered up his books and papers as Bryan approached him.

"Well, Bryan. I didn't expect to find you in my class."

"I haven't seen you at the gym. I hope I didn't scare you off."

Todd smiled and put a hand on his shoulder. "Not at all. I had to change the time I worked out, and we must have missed each other."

Bryan's brow furrowed as he realized that taking class from a professor he'd bottomed for wouldn't be a good idea. "I should probably drop this class."

Todd raised his eyebrow, again. "Why?"

"Isn't it a problem that we messed around?"

"Not for me. I expect you to work hard in this class. Of course, I could probably extend my office hours if you wanted to stop by and get a private workout."

Bryan smiled. "Or maybe the steam room."

Todd laughed. "Well, this *is* an art class. You can do an extra credit assignment on the art found in swirling steam. Let's go do some research."

"This is gonna be a great quarter. I can introduce you to my steam room study buddy, Tony."

They walked out of the classroom and headed for the gym.

# BIRTHDAY WORKOUT

## Jeff Mann

Looking like a lumberjack in plaid flannel shirt, denim jacket, jeans and work boots, Mike's axe-splitting wood beside his farmhouse when I arrive. He smiles and waves, then bends to his task again. I park my truck, climb out and simply stand there for a long moment, admiring the movement of his broad shoulders and lean hips as he labors. Way back in high school, when he was a football jock and I was a shy bookworm, I had a raving crush on Mike Lowry. I still can't believe we met again after several decades apart. I still can't believe we've been lovers since last spring.

"Sunny now, but it's supposed to flurry tonight," says Mike, stopping to wipe sweat from his brow. "Thought we could snuggle by a nice fire after dinner. Wanna help me lug in a few loads?" He gestures to the substantial pile of neatly split wood his efforts have generated. "I'll give you a reee-ward later," he adds, blessing me with one of his gleaming catfish grins.

"I'll bet you will. You look like the Platonic Ideal of the Sexy Country Boy in that outfit. Let's get the groceries in first."

Mike and I work side by side in silence, filling first the
fridge, then the wood-boxes. It's very quiet this far out in the
country: nothing but Madam's Creek purling before the farmhouse, morning wind in the trees' bare limbs, and the rapping
of woodpeckers up the hill. I love the isolation this narrow West
Virginia valley provides, the way the steep, November-leafless
slopes shelter and surround us.

Mike heaves the last armload of wood onto the porch, then
turns and embraces me. "Damn, Buck buddy. I really missed
you." Standing on tiptoes, he gives my goateed chin a quick kiss.

"Feeling's more than mutual," I say, kissing his brow and
patting his curvaceous rump. "The reading tour was fun. Those
Bay Area folks bought a lot of books. But I'm glad to be home.
Had to make it back for your birthday, right? The big four-oh?"

"Birthday?" Mike tries to look confused. "What you talking
about?"

"So does that mean you don't want all the birthday gifts
in my truck cab? Or that down-home feast I'm gonna cook?"
Bending, I nuzzle his black beard. "Or the hot scene I got
planned?"

"Gifts? Feast? Hot scene? Yum. Yes to all."

"Yum is right." I squeeze Mike's buttcheeks and nip gently
at his nose. He chortles, hugging me harder. I cup the back of
his head, pulling him closer. We share a long, sloppy kiss, then
another, then another. I can feel his hard-on against my thigh.

"Damn, Buck. Damn. I fucking *ached* for you," Mike gasps
in a brief pause during which his mouth isn't jammed full of my
tongue. "You were gone too long. I needed you so bad."

"I ached for you too, little man. Gonna make it up to you
today. Gonna make this a birthday to remember."

More kissing ensues. Beards wet with spit, at last we pull apart.

"So, gifts, huh? Cool. Whatcha get me?" Mike says, and the
bewhiskered redneck stud suddenly becomes an eager child.

* * *

It takes us a few hours, a bag of potato chips, several beers and a good bit of frustrated profanity to decipher the directions, but by early afternoon we're done with the assembly. Set on rubber gym mats, three new weight benches gleam in the sunlight filling Mike's spare bedroom. One's for chest presses, one's for preacher curls and one's for deltoid work.

"This is too much, Buck," Mike says, placing dumbbells in the weight rack while I slip metal plates and collars onto both ends of the barbell. "A whole damn home gym? How much did all this cost?"

"Don't worry about it. You know I inherited a good bit. I had no idea what I was going to get you till you started grousing about how that West End gym you like had closed. Think of it as an investment in our future," I say, squeezing the bulge of his right biceps. "I can only benefit by keeping you fit, right? God knows I'm addicted to that muscled little frame of yours."

Grinning, Mike flexes. "Yeah. Okay. Well, thanks then. I love it! I always wanted me a home gym. Let's break it in. How about we work out some?"

"How about *you* work out some while I finish this beer and watch? How about you get naked first?"

"Whoa. Work out naked?"

"Why not? I promised you a hot scene. Might as well get started. Strip for me."

"God, I love it when you tell me what to do." Grinning, Mike unbuttons his flannel shirt. Beneath, he's wearing a tight white A-shirt. He tugs it over his head, exposing well-defined pecs coated with dark hair.

"Damn. You have the torso of a demigod, boy."

Mike winks. "Glad you like what you see, Sir." Soon he's unlaced and removed his work boots and socks, then unzipped his jeans and slipped them off, along with his white briefs. He stands before me naked, hands on his hips, cock semihard, dark eyes gleaming.

"Not bad for forty, huh? I love your eyes on me, Buck. I love the way you look at me. You make me feel...like I ain't so old, I guess. Like I'm still worth wanting."

"I've never wanted a man more, buddy. You warm enough?"

"Yep. The sun's really bright in here. And I'll heat up fast once I start lifting."

"Mmm, yeah. You gonna get all sweaty and musky for me?"

"Yep." Mike chuckles, scratching an armpit. "I'm already pretty ripe after chopping wood. I know how much you like that."

"Your scent's a gift. And speaking of gifts, your birthday surprises aren't done yet. Got several more lined up, straight from San Francisco's premium leather store," I say, pulling items from my duffel bag. "Let's start with your workout outfit. Put these on." I toss him first a black jockstrap and then a black leather dog collar studded with chrome rivets.

"Oh, man!" By the time Mike's pulled on the skimpy garment and buckled the collar around his neck, his cock's bulging inside the jock's pouch.

"Looks to me as if you like those." I grip his erection and massage it briefly before taking a seat in a corner armchair. "Better stretch out first, gym boy."

"Yes, Sir." Dutifully, Mike stretches pecs, biceps and triceps. He limbers up his neck, drops into a few yoga postures to loosen up his back and works through a few push-ups and sit-ups. I take in the honey-sweet show, the flex and swell of his bare chest, powerful arms and furry thighs.

"You have the most beautiful body I've ever seen," I sigh, cupping my hands behind my head. "Bench press first. Want me to spot you?"

"Naw. What you got here? One-fifty? I do that all the time."

I watch Mike, my palms sweaty and my heart beating fast, as he huffs through one set of presses, then another and then another, his hairy chest mounds tensing and relaxing. Between sets, he pants, brushing black bangs from his brow, long-lashed eyes fixed on mine.

Finished with the last set, he rests the barbell in its rack before getting to his feet. "Liking what you see?" he asks with a cocky grin.

"What do you think?" I say, pulling my dick out of my jeans and jacking it. "On your hands and knees, mountain boy. Get on over here and suck me. I have a big birthday load waiting for you."

"Yes, *Sir.*" Mike crawls across the mat to my feet. He licks the tip of my cock, flicks his tongue up and down the shaft, then deep-throats me. For long, sweet minutes he sucks me hard, his lips a taut grip, his head bobbing in my lap while I run my fingers through his thick hair, take sips of beer and savor the mounting pleasure.

"Damn, you're good at that. Wuuhhff! That's enough. You already got me close," I say, pushing him off. "You get to choose, cock-hound. You want that load up your ass or down your throat?"

Mike stands. Wiping his mouth, he straddles my lap and grinds his rump against my groin. "I want you up my butt, ass-hound. Deep up inside me. Please. Please, Buck? I need you to pound me like there's no tomorrow. I need you to split me in half," Mike says. His brown eyes are solemn, his voice deep and hoarse with need.

"Just what I wanted to hear." I wrap my arms around him and we indulge in another bout of hard kissing before I move my attentions lower. First I lift his arms and feast on his salty, smelly pits, lapping and groaning with delight. "Wood-splitting sweat *and* workout sweat? God, you smell and taste so good."

Next I press my face into the rich hair coating his chest. I cup his thick pecs in my palms, kneading them roughly, then focus on his nipples. When we met, they were small, hard to find in such a dense thicket of fur, but after months of my brutal devotions, they're more prominent, pink buds I adore with tongue and teeth.

"Damn, Mike, I'm addicted to your nips," I growl. "I could suck on these sweet little treasures all damn night."

"Yeah. Yeah. Do it. Suck 'em raw. Make 'em hurt," Mike grunts, gripping my head and pressing his chest against my mouth. "Get 'em good and sore, Sir."

"Count on it. Got something special just for that."

From my pocket I slip them out, the black plastic clamps I bought at Mr. S. Mike grips my shoulders, wincing and stiffening, as I apply them to his nipples. "Ohhh, yeah," he gasps. When I twist them, he trembles, lifts his head and emits an almost mournful moan.

"Uuuhhhhhh! Ohhh, *yeah*. Oh man. Fuck! Fuck, that hurts good."

"Like that, huh?" I ask, biting his shoulder and neck. With one hand, I tug on the clamps; with the other, I play with the fine hair in the crack of his ass.

"Oh yeah. Oh yeah." Mike leans forward to give me better access and begins kissing me again. I brush a fingertip over his hole.

"Clean down here?" I murmur.

"Yeah. Yes, Sir. I cleaned out just before you came. Just in case..."

"Just in case I decided to overpower you, rope you up and rape you?" I tug hard on a clamp. Mike jolts and whimpers. He bows his head and groans.

"Yeah. Oh, yeah. I need all that so bad. I need roped and raped, Sir."

"Give me a little more show first," I say, nudging him off my lap. "Workout's not done yet."

Obediently, Mike stands.

"Dumbbells now," I order, stroking my exposed hard-on. "Chest flies."

Mike fetches two forty-five-pound dumbbells, lies on the bench and begins. Instantly his face distorts.

"Fuck! This makes the clamps hurt even worse!"

"So I've heard." My chuckle's deliberately wicked. "A leather top at Mr. S gave me all sorts of ideas for this scene."

"Oh fuck!" Mike's grimace deepens as he works through more repetitions.

"Can't do it? Want me to take them off?"

"Naw! I can do it." Mike closes his eyes and grits his teeth.

"Yeah? You gonna do it for me?"

"Yes, Sir. Yes, Sir! For you!"

"Good boy." I lift my beer in a toast to Mike, and then take a big swig.

After three sets, Mike's eyes are moist but his jock's still bulging. He drops the dumbbells onto the mat and stands. I finish my beer and stand as well.

Mike wraps his arms around my waist and leans into me. Quivering, he presses his face against my shoulder. "Thanks, Buck. Thanks, Sir," he murmurs.

"For what, boy?" I tousle his hair and cup his furry buttocks in my hands.

"For taking care of me. For making me suffer. For...for giving me my body back."

"Body back? You're sounding like a redneck philosopher, bud."

Mike's laugh is soft and sheepish. "I just mean...all those years I was married, those years I was fucking around with guys in rest stops...and shitty places like that...and then with leather

Tops I didn't really care about…it's like I didn't have a body, didn't…have a heart or a life…till you came back to town… and we…and you started touching me the way…the way you are now."

"Touching you is a privilege. Touching you and tasting you, it's the sweetest…" I clear my throat. "Damn, Mike, what kind of life would I have if…if we hadn't…"

"If we hadn't met again? Christ, I don't even wanna think about it."

We fall silent. For a few minutes we stand together in the fading sunlight. Outside, the wind picks up, soughing in the big spruce shading the house.

"Time for biceps and triceps," I say, squeezing his jock pouch and slapping a buttcheek. "Once you're done, I have another set of birthday surprises for you."

"More? Damn. You really went all out."

"The best is yet to come," I say. "But first, I want to see those big butch arms of yours pumped up." Gently, I fondle his still-clamped nipples. "It's really going to hurt when you have to push these pretty little tits against the preacher curl pad. Want me to take off the clamps?"

"Naw. Not yet." Mike takes a deep breath. "You know I like to prove myself to you and show you how much I can take."

Chuckling, I take a seat. "Yep. And I love that about you. My rough-'n'-tough mountain man. God, you look hot in that jock. Okay, Mr. Endurance, get to it."

As predicted, Mike's handsome face distorts with pain during the preacher curls. He does three sets nevertheless, emitting little whimpers that only get me harder. He moves on to triceps extensions, then deltoid presses, then standing biceps curls. In panting pauses between sets, he sucks my cock, and I tenderly suck his tortured nipples.

"That's it for my usual workout," Mike says, racking the

dumbbells. His face is flushed, his arms swollen with effort.

"Jesus, Mike. You're a musky miracle," I murmur, my gaze ranging over him. "Yeah, that's enough. Stretch out now."

Glistening with sweat, Mike does as he's told. Jacking myself, I breathe in his strong scent and relish the lyrical movements of his moist limbs.

"I'm done, Sir," Mike says, standing after a final set of push-ups. "Now what?"

"Let me see your asshole."

Mike turns his back to me. He bends over the arm pad of the preacher curl. His asscheeks, framed by the jock's black straps, are furry marvels. When he spreads them, I can make out, inside his butt-cleft's dark forest, that pink and puckered place I so cherish, that intimate entry that holds for me such pleasure and such wonder.

"Tie me, Buck," Mike whispers, clenching his hole with invitation. "Please tie me up. I need tied so, so bad. Tie me up and use me. Tie me up and use me hard. Please. Please, Buck. Please."

"Christ," I sigh. "I am the luckiest man on earth." Rising, I fetch black nylon rope from my duffel bag. "Hands behind your back."

A couple of minutes, a couple of cow-hitch knots, and I've bound Mike's hands behind him and cinched his elbows together. Head bowed, he slumps, sighing and shaking, over the inclined pad.

"Feel good?" I ask, tightening the last knot, then stroking his muscled back.

Mike tugs at his bonds and flexes his arms. "Christ, yes. Thank you. Thank you."

"You're so damn beautiful like this. Want me to make love to your hole now?" I say, running a finger along his buttcrack.

Mike flexes his buttocks and lifts his hips. "Yes. Oh, yes! Please. Please, Sir. Please."

I fall to my knees behind him. I brush my beard over his ass and breathe in his scent. I lick his crack, moistening the dense fur there. I bury my face between his buttocks and feast on his hole till he's whining, writhing and bucking back against my beard.

"Fuck me, Buck. Fuck me, Sir," Mike pleads. "I need you inside me so damn bad."

"Pushy bottom." I stand, grip his hips and rub my stiff crotch against his crack.

"Put it in me. Put it in me, dammit!" Mike turns his head and glares, his hands clenched into fists. "Stop teasing me. Ram it in me!"

"I think you need to shut up." I give Mike's ass a sharp slap before fetching more items from my bag. For a few snarling seconds, he gives me the struggle he knows I savor, but soon I've forced the camo bandana into his mouth and knotted it behind his head, muffling his protests.

"Not done yet, bad boy," I say, threading a long length of black rope three times between his lips and around his head before knotting it. "There you go," I say, satisfied with both my handiwork and his well-gagged, well-trussed helplessness. "And now for your birthday spanking. Forty years, forty whacks."

Again Mike puts up some resistance—heightening the intensity between us the way a whetstone hones a blade—but soon I'm on the bench with my boy over my knees, slapping his ass hard while he moans, yelps and curses. By the time I stop, his buttcheeks are bright pink and hot to the touch.

"Here's a little of what you wanted," I say, spitting into Mike's crack and moistening his hole. He stiffens, heaving a series of baritone groans as I ease a wet forefinger inside him. For a long time, I finger-fuck him steadily and tenderly. He rocks upon my lap and grunts with bliss, mumbling, "Thank you, Sir" again and again against his layered gag, his satiny tunnel tensing and throbbing around my finger.

Pulling out, I haul Mike to his feet, drag him to the guest bed and push him down upon it. There, I slip off his jock-strap, then position him on his back, his calves resting on my shoulders. I push two fingers inside him, massaging his prostate while fondling his clamped tits and jacking his cock. I edge him cruelly, bringing him close again and again. He thrusts into my fist, cursing with frustration, begging me to bring him off.

"Ah, no. This scene isn't done yet." Chuckling, I slip my finger from his pulsing passage and lower his legs. While we've been caught up in erotic rapture, the air's gone chilly and sunlight's receded from the room.

I kiss the silvery patch of beard on Mike's chin, then climb off the bed. "I always lose track of time when you're trussed and naked, boy. It's like the world doesn't exist when you're in my arms. I really need to start your birthday dinner soon. But first," I say, rummaging through my duffel bag, "one last gift."

Mike watches me—brown eyes gleaming with anticipation, white teeth gritting his rope-and-bandana gag—as I lube up the black rubber plug.

"You want this up your butt bad, don't you?" I say, smiling down at him.

"Uhhh-*huh*." Mike grins around his gag.

"On your belly. Spread your thighs. Right. Good boy."

I lube up his hole, then nudge the plug between his buttocks and push, steadily, slowly. Mike's so eager to have it inside him that the process takes only a few pained grunts and a few patient moments. Abruptly, the plug slips past his sphincter and slides into place. Mike lifts his head and moans. Flexing his taut buttocks, he begins to hump the bed.

"Like that?"

Mike responds with a vigorous nod and another deep moan. I roll him onto his back, work the plug around, and suck his cock. When he starts to get close, pounding my face in earnest, I pull off.

"Pleeeee!" is Mike's gagged attempt at "Please!"

"Naw. Not time for you to cum yet." Smiling, I help my pent-up captive to his feet. "How about you keep me company while I cook?"

As predicted, snow flurries begin just before dusk. Through the steamy kitchen window, I can see flakes swirl by along the wind. The kitchen is warm, though, and full of delicious scents: German chocolate cake cooling on the counter, chili con carne simmering on the stove, and a musky captive collared and hog-tied at my feet.

For the past two hours I've cooked, and for the past two hours Mike, fighting his bonds and grumbling into his gag, has given me the splendid show I've craved. His tits are still clamped, his ass still plugged, his cock and balls tied with a soft leather thong. His wrists and ankles are tethered together behind him so tightly he can only move with great difficulty. Bound this way for so long, he's sore, exhausted and in real pain. I can tell from that strained expression on his face, the moist pleading in his eyes, the furrows in his brow and the ragged way he grunts as he struggles to shift onto his side. But he hasn't asked to be freed. He's taking it because he knows how much I enjoy having his powerful body powerless, how much I treasure his bound and gagged vulnerability. Mike's suffering is dedicated to me.

"All that's left to do is cornbread," I say, sipping my Lord Calvert. I nudge his bearded chin with my cowboy boot, then gently press the boot's sole against his cheek. "You're really hurting, aren't you?"

Mike looks up at me. For a few seconds, we simply gaze into each other's eyes. Finally, he shrugs.

"Tell me the truth."

Mike bites down on his gag, exhales and nods.

"Thank you, Mike," I say. "Thank you for your surrender. For giving yourself up to me. It means so much, *so* much to have you like this. To see you lie there and struggle and try to get loose and know you can't. To see you suffering like a slave at my feet, knowing your life is in my hands, that you depend on me for your welfare, your future and your freedom. I own you, don't I?"

Mike musters a weak smile. He nuzzles my boot and nods.

"And you own me," I say, finishing my drink. Dropping onto my knees, I unknot the rope connecting Mike's wrists to his ankles. He stretches his long-constricted legs, whimpering with deep discomfort and relief. I untie his ankles, massage his thighs and calves, then help him to his feet. Legs shaking, he leans against me for support. I take him in my arms, kissing his gagged mouth and bearded cheek again and again.

"How about I take my belt to your beautiful butt, then treat you to the ass-pounding of your life? Would you like that?"

Mike's response is distorted but intelligible. "Hell, yes," he mumbles, brow bumping mine. "Hell, yes. Hell, yes. Hell, yes."

Bent over the preacher curl pad, Mike bellows and jolts, straining against the ropes still binding his wrists and elbows behind him, jerking against the additional ropes I've added to fasten him down to the bench. Beneath my belt, the pale, fur-covered curves of his ass, already pink after his birthday spanking, achieve a rich crimson splotched with bruises.

I beat him till he sobs. Dropping the belt, I twist his long-clamped nipples until his sobs deepen and tears course down his face. Then I strip off my clothes, ease out Mike's butt plug, and shove my cock into him. Mike winces and gasps. Writhing and nodding, he bucks his eager butt back against me. I wrap an arm around his trussed torso, press myself against him, grip his cock and start up a steady ass-pounding. After hours of sexual buildup, it takes us both less than a minute to shoot.

"That was quite the howling you made when I finally took those clamps off your tits. Another reason to call you 'cock-hound,' huh?"

"Guess so." Mike chuckles, nestling back against my chest. "I loved it when you sucked on 'em so hard right afterward."

After an hour's worth of luxurious post-cum nap, Mike and I are spooning beneath quilts in the master bedroom. On the hearth, a wood fire flickers and cracks. Outside, November night is falling, snow flurries continue their bleak necessities and wind soughs through spruce.

"You felt so good inside me, Buck. All that plug did was make me horny as hell for you to put your prick up in me. That was a plowing to remember. A birthday to remember. Man, I can't believe I'm forty." Mike heaves a sigh, plucking at his chin. "Damn gray in my beard."

"You may be forty, but you're hotter than ever," I say, kneading his rope-chafed wrists. "Every time I feel like whining about my age, I think about all the guys in my youth who died of AIDS, and that puts things in perspective. I may be forty-one, but, God, I'm thankful for all I've been given. I never thought I could feel so much passion again or care for a man so deeply. We wasted two decades apart, Mike. I don't want to waste any more time."

"Glad to hear you say that." Mike fumbles beneath his pillow and retrieves a little box. Rolling over, he hands it to me. "You've been giving me gifts all day, so now it's my turn. Here ya go."

"What you got there?" I open it. Inside are two matching silver rings etched with Celtic knots.

"My God. Are these...?"

"Wedding rings. Despite the fact that this damn backward state won't let us get married. Thought you'd like the knots. Sorry I couldn't afford gold."

"Jesus, Mike. Wedding rings? Really?"

"Really." Mike grabs my hand. "So, will you marry me? If not in the eyes of the law, in the eyes of God?"

"Wow. I can't believe it."

"Believe it. So, bud, yes or no? You gonna stick around to rope and rape your bad boy?" Mike gives me another one of those broad catfish grins that stole my heart twenty-some years ago. "Keep the ole redneck cock-hound in line? Treat my butt right?"

"To quote a certain hairy and handsome captive, 'Hell, yes!'" I squeeze his hand and kiss him hard on the mouth. "Hell, yes."

"I figured you couldn't resist my charms," Mike replies with a long-lashed wink. "This bigger one's yours." He slips the silver circle onto my left ring finger.

"And here's yours," I say, sliding the smaller ring onto his hand.

"So I guess we're husbands now," Mike says, pressing his palm to mine. In the hearth-light, the matching bands of silver glint.

"Guess so," I say, interlocking his fingers with mine. "I am one lucky man."

"Me too, Buck. I feel so safe with you. I love you so much."

"I love you too, Mike. You're one tight-assed dream come true." Reaching over, I give his swollen nipples gentle tugs.

"Ohhh, yeah. You got 'em good and sore," he groans, leaning forward to kiss me. Our tongues meet and probe, wrestle and flicker together. Wrapping an arm around him,

I pull him closer. I give his stiffening cockhead a few strokes, then slip my right forefinger between his asscheeks and rub his lube-sticky hole.

"Ummm. Uh-huh! Yep. Yep. Put it in me."

"Again? It's getting late, frisky boy." Grinning, I lick saliva off his bearded chin. "Aren't you hungry?"

"Yeah…" Sighing, Mike squirms against my teasing finger. "I even bought…some ch-champagne. Fancy French stuff…t-to go with dinner…to celebrate in case you said yes. B-but right now…" He angles his rump and bends his leg, allowing me to slip a knuckle up inside. "Oh, y-yeah. I'm thinking… I'm thinking…I need…I need…"

"Seems to me, husband, that you need to be butt-fucked yet again," I say, pushing my finger into him another inch. "I may be forty-one, but I'm up for it whenever you are."

"Damn. D-damn, husband. You got…my…hole so hungry. You got me addicted to how good your cock fills me up," Mike murmurs. "Yeah, *uhhh*. Keep that up, okay?"

"You bet," I say, driving my finger home and beginning a slow in-and-out thrust.

"Ummm, yeah. There ya go. That's sweet," Mike groans, quivering against me.

"Nothing sweeter. Not even cake. Sure you don't want dinner first?"

"Naw," Mike says huskily, pressing his face against my shoulder. "Food can wait. Got another hunger needs fed first. Work my hole some more, please, Sir. Then tie me belly-down to the bed, tape your underwear in my mouth, climb on top of me and screw me again. Make it sweet and slow and deep. Make it last a long time. Ride me till I'm raw, then dump another load up my ass. Please, Sir."

I kiss his cheek, watching firelight burnish his bare limbs. "You got it," I reply, working in a second finger. "Feel good?"

"Lord, yes. Lord, yes." Mike nods dreamily, stroking his cock, sighing inside the blessing our mingled bodies make. His submissive ass, slick and tight, pulses rhythmically around my fingers. "I can feel your heart," I whisper. As if in answer, the hearth logs flare up in brief and fiery triumph.

# GYM FRIENDS

### Fox Lee

Anyone who tells you he likes going to the gym is a liar. He may get off on the endorphins, he may love the rush, but only true freaks love the gym. I hate the gym. I hate driving there after a day of work; never mind that I work from home I still hate it. I hate the stupid outfit I wear, the special shoes I had to buy and the drinks they sell at the bar. Bar my ass, it's a place for the actor/barista to spy on us then dish over soy crap lattes.

The worst part is that I'm still at the age where I don't have to go to the gym. I'm fit without trying, the blessing of being Asian. Call it a stereotype, but statistics don't lie. Unfortunately, one day being trim won't be easy and I don't want to wait until then to get used to making myself unhappy. If I were coupled and deeply in love, I would let myself get a little soft. Alas, love hasn't found me yet. So here I am, at the gym, miserable.

Some info on me: I'm average height (when any man says that it means he's a little short) with long dark hair and Thai skin. Think coffee with light cream Thai. I've been told I pass for straight, which is supposed to be a compliment, but honestly dating would be easier if I didn't spook the nice gay boys. Hence I go to a gay gym. At the moment, I'm working on my legs and trying to ignore the trickle of sweat running down my ass. That's when I see him. Skinny. Tall. Japanese. Oh Buddha forgive me, but I love Japanese men too much to ever become a monk. Sorry Mom (long story). He's on the treadmill, his legs lost in his baggy basketball shorts. I love him. I'm going to spend the rest of my life with him. I wonder what his name is?

Within three weeks, I have rearranged my schedule to match sexy Japanese guy's. He keeps to himself and I'm shy, but there's no reason to think he's an asshole. I maintain a polite distance, never let on that I spend my workout imagining his skinny ass naked. What his hole looks like stretched out and wet, what his teeth feel like clumsily bumping my dick. I save my energy for home, where I beat off so hard my dick calls a lawyer the next morning.

Forget my dick, back to sexy Japanese guy. I'm so fixated on him I almost miss the red flag. Finally it clicks, every time I see him at the gym he's running like he's trying to escape a fart. It's the only thing he does, no weights, no machines. When he looks ready to pass out he takes a shower and goes home. This is all very mysterious and hot, but after a while I get worried. He's losing a lot of weight, looking haggard. Cute skinny is one thing, but my future husband is wasting away and that won't do.

I ask around to see if anyone knows him or his story. Maybe he's getting over a flu, and there's nothing to worry about. Maybe he's on drugs, and a lost cause. The tenderer among us debate whether to say anything. My closest friends, four bears that would scare me if I didn't know them so well, are blunt. Someone has to say something they decree, he's going too far.

"If he wants to kill himself, he can do it at home," my friend Rick says. "I don't want to see that shit."

We draw condoms. I get the non-lubricated one. The Trojan has spoken.

I'm not happy. Why do I have to be the one to alienate the hot Japanese guy? I like him. I have warm, squishy feelings about him on an hourly basis. Sadly, that very reasoning works against me. If I love him so much, why won't I talk to the guy? I wait until he's in the locker room, freshly showered with his pants on, and move before he gets his shirt on. He might never come near me again, so I have to make the most of the moment.

"Hey," I say as I sit down. Because all great speeches start with a pointless address. "Can I talk to you about something?"

"Sure." He leans away a little.

"I've been noticing you working out. It's really impressive; I would die if I ran that fast."

"Thanks."

He calms down, resumes putting his socks on.

"But you're getting a little..." I sigh. "Oh fuck it. You're starting to look like a stick figure dude, and it's a shame to do that to a hot body."

I wait for him to yell at me, or shove me off the bench. Instead he gets up and goes to the mirror next to the scale. He stares at himself a long time, then gets this look in his eyes that breaks my heart.

"How long has it been this bad?" he asks.

"It's not bad. But you're headed there. You know you're not fat, right?"

He laughs. It makes his eyes look incredible.

"Fat? I'm about two hundred pounds from fat!" He sits back down, closer than before. "I don't run to lose weight, I run because I'm angry at my ex-boyfriend. He cheated on me, and acted like I was the asshole when I left him."

"That's it?" I probe.

"That's it. One bad breakup and I turn into Forrest Gump."

"Maybe you can take a dance class."

"Too much thinking."

"You miss him that much?"

"Like I'll miss the STD he gave me."

"Ah." I contemplate this. "Curable?"

"Yeah. Although I'm going to have to go back to make sure that's all he gave me. I mean I don't think he gave me anything bad, but who knows? We skipped the condom a couple nights, and it's all I can think about when I can't sleep."

This is not sexy talk, so why do I want to throw him down and lick every inch of his body like some giant cat? I put my hand on his back. *There, there,* it's meant to say. *I'm not thinking of how your nipples taste, I promise.* I can smell his skin, which is so clean from the shower it almost glows.

"Do you want to go out for coffee?" I ask.

Coffee is safe. Coffee is not the drink of sex perverts and sociopaths. Those people drink tea.

"Caffeine after a workout?"

"I won't tell."

"I would like that," Sexy  Guy says. I have missed the window to ask for his name. "But I can't. I mean I'm not ready."

"I get it. But if you would never ever say yes, please tell me now. I mean, being polite is great, but in this case rejection is better."

He's surprised. Humble guys are the best. "I would love to have coffee with you," he said. "Eventually."

"Then consider me on standby."

"That's not fair." He kisses me on the cheek and my cock wilts. "But you're a nice guy."

"How do you know I'm a nice guy?"

"You want to take me out for coffee, instead of offering me

your dick as consolation for my breakup." He shakes my hand.
I want to throw up. "I'm Tai."

"Unlikely," I counter.

"It's short for Taisan."

"I'm Pakon."

"Laos?"

"Thai."

"Japanese."

I smile. "I know."

"Is my sword showing?"

Bless his heart; he's not trying to be cute. I'm assuming he
means a Japanese short sword, unlike the long sword I've seen
between his legs.

"I'm good with accents," I tell him. "Do you want to work
out together? I'm on the edge as it is, and you need a second
pair of eyes."

"On the edge?"

"I don't like the gym. A partner would help me stick with
my workouts."

"Sure." Tai smiles at me. "You can keep me from melting
away to nothing."

"It will be my pleasure."

He gives me a knowing look, and we exchange numbers. I
tell myself he'll back out, but he doesn't. We meet up four times
a week, one more than I would on my own. There's no flirting,
at least not on his end, but over time I realize I really do like
him. The inside, I mean. He's funny, and really smart. And his
ass is amazing.

Despite the lack of coy looks or come-hither glances, I refuse
to give up hope. And whenever I'm sure I'm in the friend zone,
I get little hints that all is not down the shitter. Like when Tai
tells me his STD check came back all clear, a sultry hint that he
might soon be on the market. Juice Barista agrees with me. I'm

not one to gossip, but Tai leaves before I do and way before my boner goes down, so drinking something terrible is like a cold shower. I don't specifically mention the STD of course, just like I don't tell Barista how much his drinks suck.

"He likes you," Barista said. "He likes you a lot."

"I hope so."

"I see how he looks at you, all hearts and rainbows."

"Can you make that gayer? I almost thought about boobs for a second there."

"Listen to me; he broke up with a rotten guy. It will be a while before he wants to date someone like you."

"Like me?"

"Oh love," Barista sighs. "I know you think you're a bad boy, with the motorcycle and the almost beard I keep telling you to shave, but you're adorable. You're the kind of guy that gets stuck in the friend zone so fast your dick gets whiplash."

"Your apologies suck. And I know all about the zone. The zone can kiss my ass."

"Not a bad idea."

"What?"

"Sucking. Ass kissing. The boy is in pain, maybe he needs some stress relief."

"And that will make him go out with me?"

"Go out with you, that's precious."

"Go to hell." I stick my tongue out.

"That's the spirit! But don't forget to work the balls."

The next day, in front of me, Barista takes Tai aside and asks if he's ready to get back on the bull. I drag Tai away and shoot daggers at the guy who will no longer be getting tips from me.

"Does he mean what I think?" Tai asks.

"He's not known for being subtle."

"You know, your friends are always smiling at me."

I want to crawl into a hole. "They just smile, right?"

"No. At least once a week one of them tells me what a great guy you are. Usually at the urinal."

"Great."

I'm touched, in a way that makes me want to personally kill every one of them. I should mention that my gym is popular with mature gay men. Hairy-chested, muscled, bearded guys who treat me like a baby brother. There's no sexual tension. I'm way too hairless they tell me, which is good since more than a few of them could snap me like a cheap plastic toy, which makes the whole killing them thing more difficult.

"They said you have excellent hygiene," Tai says. "And your dick is cut but very responsive."

"Did they talk about my asshole, too?"

"No, but they mentioned what you want to do to mine."

"I never said anything about yours!"

"So you aren't a top?"

"Of course I'm a top!" I yell, loud enough for people to hear. I hate my friends. I hope they all get anal warts.

My hatred grows as they continue to promote me through the month. Tai lets me know the most embarrassing reports. How I can shoot really far, which isn't true and if it is who cares? How I'm generous with my tongue, which is true. Then they start outright lying. I love being spanked, they tell him. I wear women's panties and need to be called a nasty school-girl. Perhaps out of pity, Tai softens and our workouts become more intimate. We flirt, and joke around a lot. Soon I'm the one getting looks from my gym friends. I get the feeling that if I ever do get to sleep with Tai, I'm going to be expected to hang the semen-stained sheet from my window.

When they run out of shit to say, they cut to the chase. Which is to say, they send the representative bear. Rick corners me in the shower, just as I'm about to wash my crack. He was the first to adopt me when I started at the gym, and always took a very personal interest in my love life. He said it was every older gay man's duty to pick a young man who needed him and help the youth be all he could be.

"Dude, you have to seal the deal."

"I'm glad my sex life is so interesting to you. Makes me wonder about yours."

"First, you have no sex life, so it can't be interesting." Rick lathers shampoo into his beard then tilts his head back to let the shower wash it out. "Secondly, my sex life would scorch your foreskin off."

"Don't have one," I say. "But nice to know you don't look at me like a cheap piece of steak."

"I'm being colorful, you prick. You think I haven't looked at your cock and balls? I have. Nothing to write home, but nothing to be ashamed of."

"Mr. Rick, are you trying to seduce me?"

"He has an ex, right?"

"Don't we all? No wait, you have to date for that."

"Will you shut up and listen? He broke up not long ago; he could still wind up with the guy. If you want him, you have to claim him."

"He hates his ex. And I'm not peeing on him."

"They all say that! Were you born gay yesterday? And who said anything about peeing?"

"Look, I want to. But he's delicate, and I don't want to scare him off."

"Delicate my left nut. Get his pants off, drop to your knees, make him forget he ever dated the other douche."

"You are such a cutie," I coo. "How is it you aren't married already?"

"Don't ask me," Rick looks down and shakes his substantial cock. "Ask him."

I get on my knees and give his dick a stern look.

"Mr. Wang. Have you been giving Rick trouble?"

"Yes, I have," Rick's meat admits. "Bring me a hairy cub to suck the naughty out of me!"

I laugh so hard I nearly slip and break my ass bone. Rick leaves me to my shower and joins the other burly guys in the locker room. Knowing them, they won't be getting dressed anytime soon. It's a parade of cocks in there, a sacred tradition of any good gay gym. Why wait to be old, like straight boys do, when you can parade your junk around during the prime of your life? I brush off Rick's advice, and go back to my asscrack. What did he know about lasting love, anyway? This was the guy who said never eat breakfast with someone who's had your dick in his hole.

My confidence doesn't last, and Rick's words get to me. Rick could be right; Tai could be in love with his ex. People make stupid decisions all the time. I've never seen the guy, so it's easy to imagine him as everything I'm not. Ripped, tall, a glowering hunk of pure sex. If Tai doesn't take me up on a coffee date soon, I'm going to start thinking the worst. Maybe I should suck his cock, everyone likes his cock sucked.

I knew I did, though I haven't had the pleasure since I found out Tai was available. Nor have I had anything else, at least not from a hand that wasn't my own, since I don't want Tai to find out and think I've moved on. Meanwhile my friends are all happy with their sex lives, and it's starting to piss me off. There's Rick, the stud who has men lining up to bask in his musk. The three musketeers Bill, Anton and Sean, a trio in the gym and the bedroom. They even owned a house together, with the biggest bed I've ever seen. I passed out in it once, at a party, and woke up surrounded by snoring bears. It was like being in a fur womb.

What the hell is wrong with me that I'm struggling to get

one guy? Maybe I smell when I work out. Maybe that time I thought Tai didn't notice me fart he actually did. I'm not ugly. I'm not boring. I am, however, turning into a neurotic old woman worrying what Tai thinks of me. No gay man wants to fuck an old woman. The next night I go to the gym early, and towel up for a preemptive shower. When Tai gets there, I assure myself, I will only smell of manhood, cock and sexy, superclean balls.

He must have come in right after me. The gym showers are tucked away from the locker room at an angle; you can't see anything beyond the corner. But you can hear plenty. Tai isn't alone. He's arguing with someone, it doesn't take me long to figure out who and why.

"What do you think you're accomplishing?" Tai demands. "I don't want to see you. Stalking me isn't going to change anything!"

"I'm not stalking; I bought a day membership so I could talk to you!"

"We talked! Many times!"

"Maybe you need to listen!"

"I don't have to listen; I don't want to be with you!"

"I made a mistake, are you fucking perfect?"

"You didn't make a mistake. A mistake is an action. You are a man whore. A throbbing cock that never rests until it finds some stranger's ass to bareback!"

There's a slap, and I hurry out of the showers to see who got hit and find Tai with a palm print on his face, with a guy who looks like he was rejected from the Jersey Shore for being too much of a douche. I grab Jersey douche by the shirt, and drag him behind me back to the shower. He loses his footing, and stumbles to reclaim it in time to get thrown against the shower wall and blasted with cold water. I pull his pants down, underwear too, and slap his ass so hard I'm surprised the skin doesn't break. I wrench the shirt over his head, bend him over, and slap him again. Tai stays at the corner of my vision and, based on the peek I get, shock is too vanilla a word for what he's feeling. I'm about to pull his ex's head up, punch him in the nose and call it a night, when my friends come around the corner. They gently wind their way around Tai to line up a few feet behind his ex.

"So?" Rick asks. "You boys going to fight or what?"

Bill and Anton wave, they're the gentlemen of their little group, and Tai's ex shrieks as I tackle him to the shower floor. I've taken Judo since I had hair on my nuts, the start of my feelings for Japanese men, and while I was never a champion I can clean up the place with a guy like this. He has no moves, no fighting background. I forget that Tai is nearby, all I remember is the mark on his face and who put it there. I wrench the ex's arm behind his back and punch him in the stomach. He belches, loudly, and I recoil.

"God, do you live on kale shakes or something?" I ask.

He goes for my legs; I flip him into the air and watch him slam into the ground. He lumbers to his feet, red faced and calling me every nasty name in the book.

"Hey," Rick yells, "he's hard!"

I look down and see an erection I could run a flag up. I smack it, and precum flows out like lava. The ex has a funny look in his eyes; with a flash his hands are on my dick tugging it toward his open mouth. The bears sweep in, and Bill and Sean grab his arms and Anton takes his legs.

"Now that isn't nice," Rick says. "You think my baby boy here wants to waste his dick on someone like you?"

Bill and Sean get Tai's ex onto his knees. Rick pulls out his cock, which emerges from its foreskin like a purple snake. The ex takes it without any prompting, sucks it down to the hilt. As Rick face-fucks him, Sean and Bill spread his legs so Anton can appear between them, condom on and cock ready to roll. He fingers lube into Tai's ex, who makes a sound like a cow in heat.

"He's been a bad boy," Rick says. "I think he needs his piggy poked!"

"Happy to."

Anton grips the guy's ass like he's about to break it open. I always knew he was a people pleaser. I watch him shove his cock in, high-fiving Rick as he does. Tai's ex drools; his eyes roll to the back of his head.

A hand touches my back and I nearly scream bloody murder. It's Tai, the red mark on his face faded to pink. I can hear suction sounds as his ex rides Anton's dick, sucking the cream out of Rick's on the backhand stroke.

"Umm, can I tell you something?" Tai asks.

"Sure."

"I think it's too late for coffee."

I'm crushed. But I understand, or think I do until Tai grabs me, cups my ass, and sends his tongue on a rescue mission into my mouth. I'm pried apart, fondled, slowly walked away from the minor orgy in the shower and into the locker room. I can still hear plenty: Anton is coming and Bill wants to go next.

"No way," Rick shouts. "After you fuck him his hole will be too wide for the rest of us!"

Tai lets go of my ass. He takes off his clothes. I make a mewling sound like a lost kitty. My cock looks up at me like I've lost my mind. *Man up*, it says. *It's show time.*

"Condoms?" Tai asks.

"In my locker."

Tai takes the condom I hand him, tears the wrapper open and pops the latex into his mouth. My dick follows, and I feel the latex sheath unroll to the base of my shaft. Tai reclines along the bench, naked and ready. A dollop of lube and his legs are over my shoulder. Rick is letting everyone know he's about to come, that he's going to drown "the little bitch" with his spunk. Sean warns him that the hole is tight, that Tai's ex must be a greedy little top who needs a daddy to teach him better. The air is full of romance.

"You ready?" I ask Tai.

He nods.

One thrust, and I know his ex is an idiot. Tai works my cock—muscles it, tugs it, massages it down to the balls, which bounce off his ass like I'm playing Ping-Pong. I like my nuts roughed up, but it makes me hotter and quicker to come. I bite his nipples to distract myself, which Tai likes a lot. He screams my name so loud it outdoes the shower fuckfest, and a shot of come hits my chin.

"Hey, warn a guy why don't you?" I pant.

Tai bucks in response, and grabs his dick before it shoots again. I lick come off his chest almost faster than he can make it, then pull him close to me, wary of those skinny shoulder blades getting bruised by the bench. We manage not to roll off as I discharge. I gasp, I swear, I profess undying love for Tai and the magical world beyond his amazing anus. Then, applause.

"Oh god," I close my eyes. I'm still inside Tai. Still hard actually, though there's no chance of an encore now. "Please tell me I had a stroke and they aren't behind us."

"They are," Tai kisses me. "And I love you, too."

An elderly man is pressed against the lockers. He looks shocked, but his dick says he enjoyed the show as much as anyone else.

"I think we need to run for it," I tell Tai. He agrees.

We make it out, naked but safe from whatever celebration my friends have in store. Luckily I'm parked close by. I take Tai home, move him in the next day. Another month and we'll get tested and, knock on wood, ditch the condoms.

As for the ex, he tried one more time to get back with Tai, and Tai laughed so hard he had to change his pants when he got home. When you let a quartet of bears use you like a piece of Swiss cheese you don't really get to claim changed man status. These days the cheese fuckers argue over who gets to be my best man. I have no clue; Tai and I just moved in together. But I'll tell you one thing: they're not coming on the fucking honeymoon.

# MONTGOMERY GYMNOS

## Shane Allison

When I saw Bill at the movies last night, my heart dropped into my ball sac.

"Hey man, how's it goin'? Bill asked.

"Pretty good. How you doin'?"

"Can't complain. What are you here to see?"

"*Hugo*. I was trying to decide if I wanted to see that or *Breaking Dawn*." I lied through my teeth. I had my mind set on seeing the new Scorsese movie for a week. I hate that *Twilight* shit and I can't stand talentless Kristin "Bony Bitch" Stewart.

"I think you made the right decision," Bill grinned. He was dressed from his buzz-cut flattop to his black boots in cop garb, unlike the campus security getup he used to wear. Bill had moved up in the ranks.

"I think so, too." Bill still looked the same. He had aged slightly, lost some weight, but he was still fine as hell. And that cop uniform only made him hotter. I think someone told me he was working full-time at the Tallahassee Police Department.

"All right, Bill, I'll see ya when I come out," I waved.

"Later, Shane."

Last time I saw him he almost caught me about to suck off this guy under the bathroom stalls in the Montgomery Gym showers back when he was a campus cop at Florida Southern University. Minutes before I was about to drop to my knees, I peered over my partition to see if the coast was clear and there in front of the door of the shower room stood two cops: Bill and this bald guy whom I had seen patrolling the campus. They both looked like they were not in the mood to take any shit. Bill didn't know who I was until I stepped out of the stall. Needless to say, I kept my cool.

"Bill, hey, how's it going?" I said timidly, as I sauntered up to one of the sinks to wash my hands.

"Shane," was all he said with this mean, militant look that ran across his face. I had no idea what the guy in the shitter next to me looked like until he eventually wandered out to join me at the sinks. He was cute with short, cinnamon-brown hair and a *phat* ass. Looking at him, I was pissed that we had been bothered only seconds before I was about to gobble this white boy's dick.

"What were you guys doing?" Bill asked.

"Nothing. I was just using the bathroom."

"So was I," the twink said. They looked at us knowing good and well that we weren't going to tell them what was really up. *Oh, I was just about to go down on this guy's dick before ya'll walked in.* Yeah, right. "We've been getting some complaints about suspicious behavior going on in here. You guys need to be careful." I was embarrassed that Bill suspected what I was doing or was about to do, but I had come out to him back in the day when we were ushers at this rat-infested movie theater. He was the only one who was cool with me. I did a three-month stint and hauled ass. I hated the managers, a married couple that ran the place. Bill and this guy Thaddeus were the only guys I talked to. I didn't even put in two weeks' notice. I didn't see Bill for six years before that day on campus.

I figured this old bitch who has an office located across from the gym showers was the one who called po-po. She was always sitting at her desk watching like some big ol' black buzzard. They had no choice but to let us go being that they didn't catch us doing anything. I had already been warned by someone else who cruised to be careful, the cops on campus were cracking down, coming in plainclothes and pretending to be students. They popped this guy just last week in the library shitters. I only go there as a last resort when I can't get any dick in the Bellamy bathrooms, which is where I usually frequent. They have glory holes in the stalls where guys stick their dicks through to get head. I sit on the other side where it's always best to give than to receive. I hardly ever like to get sucked. Damn, talking about this is making my dick stir.

The only thing that I couldn't stand about the Montgomery showers was that there was no time to recover if you were doing something and someone walked in. I had gotten pinched by the cops in the park a year before, so I wasn't going to take any chances. After Bill and his bald partner were done questioning us and had given us a warning, they let us go. The twink and I walked in different directions but met up later at a bench in front of the student union.

"Shit, that was close," I said.

"I know, right?"

"If they'd come in seconds later, we would probably be on our way to jail," I told him.

"Yeah. You gotta be careful. I've heard the cops have been sniffing around."

"I bet it was that old lady who told on us," I said.

"What lady?"

"This old bitch that has an office across from the showers.

Every time I go in, I see her just sitting there at her desk looking at who's going in and coming out. She's probably the one who called the cops."

"I've never seen her, but I'm glad I know that. I won't be going back there," he said.

"She's not there all the time though. You just gotta keep an eye out."

"Yeah, man, but the cops. If I get arrested, I could lose my scholarship and get my ass kicked out of school. My folks would kill me and then dig my ass back up once they found out what I got arrested for and kick my ass again."

This fool kept going on like I cared. I just wanted to suck his dick.

"Yeah, as long as you're careful, you won't get caught," I said.

"I don't think there's any such thing as being careful when you do that shit though."

He had a point.

"So we can um…go somewhere else if you want," I said.

"Naw, I'm pretty shaken up with what went down back there, man. I think I'm just gonna head out."

"Are you sure? I would love to suck your dick." The twink pulled away when I started to caress his thigh. He laughed like I was crazy to be so ballsy.

"Maybe another time, but thanks," he said. He walked off leaving me with a raging hard-on. *Well, take your ass on then. Fuck you!* I thought. I didn't think I would ever see him again, but being the tearoom queen that I am, I oughta know that they always come back. I got his dick after all in the ground-floor bathroom at Bellamy one afternoon. "Suck that cock," he kept saying.

*Slurp.*

*Slurp.*

*Slurp.*

I sucked until I made that white boy nut so fuckin' hard. He got cum all over my jeans. He didn't know it was me until I stuck my head over the wall of my stall. He smiled when he saw that it was me and then exited the bathroom. I never saw him again after that day. It's too bad, too. That was some good juicy dick. I love cruising on campus. College boys have primo boners.

I returned to Montgomery like a week later after I figured shit had died down. I kept watch for that old snitch-ass bitch that narced on me the last time. If her office door was open, I knew she was perched at her usual spot. If it was closed, I knew she was out to lunch or had taken her ass home. The day that I went to go see what was up, her office door was closed. God wanted me to get some dick that day. When I walked in, all I heard was a shower running. The stalls were vacant. I occupied the one closest to the wall, the *giving* end. I waited for like an hour. The reverberation from the shower had gotten on my nerves. There I was half-ass naked on the toilet and hard and there wasn't a dick to be had. That's one of the things I hate about cruising. Shit can be hit or miss. I got bored just sitting there. My legs were starting to fall asleep. "Fuck this," I said, and pulled up my pants. "I'm going to Bellamy. I like it there better anyway."

I stood at the sink washing my hands when I spotted this image in the mirror. This guy was standing there behind me, booty-naked and wet. My eyes zeroed in on his fat donkey dick that hung between his tan-lined legs. He looked to be in his late twenties or early thirties. All he wore was his glasses. He was balding. The hair he had left was thinning and blond. I had seen him before. I had the pleasure of sucking his pretty dick on a couple of occasions in the fifth-floor toilet in Strozier Library. I think his name was John. A fake name I figured, but whatever. The windows were fogged with steam from the shower. I turned to face him. Shower water trickled along his chest and belly, and beaded in his bushel of pubes, leaking like precum off the circumcised spout of his donkey dick. My glasses were starting to fog up like the set of windows above the showers.

"I hadn't seen you around. How are you?" John asked.

"What are you doing? You're gonna get caught." I couldn't stop cutting glances at his dick.

"It's cool. There hasn't been anyone around since I've been in here," he told me.

"Somebody still might come in though."

John was making me nervous standing there naked. He wasn't in the best of shape, but I don't mind a little chunk as long as it's in the right place, preferably the ass. I love to fuck and eat a nice bubble. John had a slight paunch, thick arms and thighs, and he had a little man-boob action coming in. John had a Seth Rogan physique before Seth Rogan went all Weight Watchers on a nigga. I was nervous as hell, but it didn't stop my dick from twitching in my jeans. I pulled my eyes from his thick cock long enough to ask, "So there hasn't been a lot of action going on in here?"

"I just got here. I haven't seen anybody." I figured if he had, he would be on his knees right now.

"I didn't know they still use these showers," I said. "I thought guys just come in here to change."

"I don't think they do, really. I was jogging and was going to go home to shower, but I didn't want to get my car seats all sweaty. I remembered these showers and came here."

He was torturing me. I was hungry for his dick. I took it in my hand and started to massage it as I ran my thumb across one of his nips. His dick was warm still from the shower, yet cool from the air that kissed it. I veered John's bulbous head to my lips and took his appendage into my mouth. His wet belly grazed against my glasses as I sucked.

*Slurp.*

*Slurp.*

*Slurp.*

I didn't care if we got caught or who saw us. All I could think about was sucking that dick. John pushed until his dick teased the rear of my throat.

"Let's hit the showers." I started to get undressed, stepping out of my sandals, dropping out of my shorts and drawers, peeling off my shirt. I followed John to the showers; pearls of water peppered his ass. I couldn't keep from looking at his taut booty. Both of our dicks were bone hard. Warm shower water pelted our bodies. We wrapped our fingers around each other's wet hard-ons.

"I want to rim your ass," I said.

"I've never had that done before, but I'm down."

I was eager to turn that ass out. John bent over. I traipsed a finger along his crack. I dropped to the balls of my knees. John's ass was point blank to my face. The gym showers were thick with steam. John's treasure was exposed. I smeared my face in.

I licked and sucked at his cherry.

*Give me that ass.* John eased onto his elbows, face pressed into the shower floor. A bolt of shock and fear shot through my chest when I glanced up from John's ass to find Bill peering from behind the tile wall, jacking his dick that hung past the copper teeth of his zipper. Bill looked to be about seven and a half, maybe eight inches with a good amount of girth to his cop dick. He stood there in silence, watching us, watching me grind my face in between John's glutes. Nothing turns me on more than being watched. The more men, the fucking better. His pale, skinhead of a partner wasn't with him. Too bad. I would have done them both.

I waved him over as I kept eating ass. Bill started to get undressed. Shit, it was about to be on and poppin'. I watched him peel off his uniform. When he dropped the metallic holster on the floor from his slim waist, it startled John. Bill undid his shirt exposing a bulletproof vest. More skin was steadily starting to show. Big powerful arms, a white cotton tee stretched over pectorals. I finger-teased John's hole as Bill stepped out of shoes and socks. A peach fuzz of hair was centered on his chest. Damn, he was fine. Don't know when was the last time I had seen a body that looked that good. Bill crept along the shower floor in front of John, who was eager to take his appendage into his mouth.

I stood up off my knees. John was primed for fucking. I was starting to prune so I shut off the shower. I straddled John, aiming my dick at his center. With a single thrust, it sank into his ass. Bill and I watched each other as we spit-roasted John from both ends. Bill's face flushed red. We were both close to shooting off. I knew Bill wouldn't hold out much longer, not with the deep-throating John was putting down on that cop cock.

*Slurp.*

*Slurp.*

I knew from experience that he wouldn't stop until he'd gotten that nut. The man is ravenous, so I wasn't surprised that he could keep up with us. The occasional moan and "Fuck yeah," echoed throughout the showers.

"Damn, this some good ass."

"Take this dick."

"Take it."

Who knows how many dicks this bottom had taken up his ass? The backs of my thighs were on fire. Fuck, I couldn't hold out any longer. As I slid out, I jerked thick streams of nut across his pimpled ass.

"Yeah."

"Yeah."

"Fuck yeah."

"Fuckin' cum."

Bill continued to work his mouth.

"Yeah. Fuck his mouth."

"Suck that big fuckin' dick."

John started sucking Bill faster.

I looked up at Bill as he thrust his slab of cop dick in John's mouth.

"Fuck his face."

"Damn, man you can suck a dick."

"Here it comes," Bill said. Before another word rolled past my lips, Bill came.

*Gulp.*

*Gulp.*

"Take that cum," I said.

Bill eased his dick out of John's mouth. John lapped up the few drops of jizz from the spout of Bill's dick before he collapsed on the floor. I was exhausted. Our dicks were limp against our thighs.

Damn that was hot.

Bill treated us like we weren't even there as he got dressed, buckling his shiny black holster back around his waist.

I stood naked before him.

"You want to um—do this on the reg?" I said in a cocky tone.

"They're gonna start cracking down hard on this place so you better stay out of here. Tell him to do the same. Better get dressed. The janitors will be by here soon to clean."

I put my clothes on, leaving John to shower off. The last time I saw him he was working at one of the bookstores on campus. I think about John sometimes, wondering if he has a lover, or has maybe converted to heterosexuality or is cruising some gym shower someplace.

* * *

Bill was outside in the lobby of the movie theater.

"How was it?"

"Good. Slow at first, but pretty good."

"My wife wants to see it, so we might try to make it by next week."

"You should. It's a cool movie," I said.

"Well, have a good night. It was good seeing you again," said Bill.

"You too. Take care."

The following week I went to Montgomery Gym. They had remodeled the building and turned the showers into a class-room. It was the end of an era. I left knowing that it was one of the hottest spots I had fucked in.

# MR. SAMPSON'S MUSCLE PALACE

## R. W. Clinger

I was a beef-head all the way and had the muscles to prove it. At twenty-three, my biceps were the size of watermelons and my abs were like speed bumps. I couldn't tell you how thick my neck was, but all my queer friends and fellow workout buddies said it looked like a barrel. All those guys loved my hulking, hairless and ripped chest, not that I blamed them. And let's not forget to mention the tube of uncut cock between my legs. The dick was almost nine inches long when it was fully erect and two inches thick. Think porn-quality stuff. Think XXX all the way. And think *ouch!* Because I knew what to do to please a man.

My boss, Dean Naylor at the *Village Herald,* was into redheads and queers, but still wouldn't provide me with a serious article to write. I would have let him bounce up and down on my dick if he gave me the John Doe murder down on 6th Street, or drug deals that were being practiced after midnight behind the First Lutheran Church on Dixie Street. But Naylor denied having an attraction to my beefy bod and fall-into green eyes;

I knew better. In the end, I got stuck with the shitty stories: favorite places to buy teacups in the city, hoarders, and a new flavor of ice cream at Renaldo's Splits & Fountain Bar.

So I was hot, a stud, and I could write. My degree in journalism was obtained at Temple. I didn't have a boyfriend, stayed away from sugar, and I liked to work out at least four times a week, sometimes five; it all depended on my schedule. And I had a great pair of balls, which almost prompted me to walk into Naylor's office, strip out of my khakis and too-small tee and show him my cut frame so he would give me an intriguing and serious article to write. The guy probably would have urinated himself with surprise at my drooping balls and thatch of thick red hair above my shaft. Saliva would have maybe dripped out of his mouth. But those actions didn't happen because I played it cool; I needed the job, the paycheck, and showed him respect.

Naylor didn't work out, but I didn't hold that against him. He was still handsome, with his firm jaw, broad shoulders, and dark scruff on his chin and cheeks.

I sat across from him at his desk, adjusted my cock and balls (for his pleasure) a few times in his presence, and listened to the story he wanted me to create.

"There's a new gym in town I want you to do a piece on, Kurt," he said, checking out the khaki outline of my private parts between my thick thighs. He licked his lips and smiled, delighted with my available goods.

"Is it Pulls and Pushes on Mercer Avenue?" I asked. The mentioned gym was thirty days old and my roommate, Mike Puller, worked there.

He shook his head, passed me a business card and said, "It's a private gym. There's no sign out front as of yet, this is how new the business is. Some of its patrons are calling the place Mr. Sampson's Muscle Palace."

I wanted to laugh but didn't. Instead, I looked down at

the black-and-white business card and saw that there was an address and nothing more. No phone number. No manager's or owner's names. No website. No witty blurb to advertise the place and lure fellow beefsters such as myself to work out there.

"I'll give you three days for a story. No later."

I accepted the writing gig, fingered the plain card and left his office so he could masturbate and unload the hard dick that he was hiding under his desk from me.

My straight roommate, a twenty-four-year-old muscled jarhead who'd spent two terms in Afghanistan, looked at the business card Naylor had given me and said, "I know the guy who runs that place."

"Mr. Sampson?"

"Darnell Sampson. He's big and black with muscles the size of planets. He has dreadlocks and a grin that will make you come inside your boxer-briefs, without the thing even being touched."

"You're fucking with me, Mike," I said, disbelieving him.

Mike was now a physical-fitness trainer and knew the right things to eat, the vitamins to take and the weights to lift. He was making a protein shake at our kitchen counter, scooping chocolate powder into a blender and talking to me. "Cross my heart. I'm telling the truth."

I checked out his well-built frame again and found his pretty-boy blond looks irresistible. He was into Nebraska cowgirls though, and I didn't stand a chance with him. There was no way of converting him to a cocksucker anytime soon, even if I was drop-dead chiseled and interested in taking care of my body.

"How do you know Darnell Sampson?" I asked.

"He came into Pulls and Pushes and tried to bribe me to join his gym. I told him I wanted to see the place before making up my mind. He said that was fine. So I checked the place out." He screwed the cap back on the plastic bottle of protein and set it aside.

"What did you think of the place?"

He nodded and winked at me. "Just your typical gym."

"What's the wink about?"

He tapped the business card I was holding and said, "Use that card to get inside and you'll find out."

I wasn't afraid of anything. Not Naylor. Not Mike. And certainly not a stranger named Darnell Sampson. To prove such a fact, I said to my roommate, "I'll do that, friend."

He laughed, but I didn't know why. Then he pressed the MIX button on his blender and continued preparing his shake.

Two nights later at seven o'clock in the evening I made my way to the address on the business card with my gym bag, judging the place a shithole from the outside. Number 982 Smithton Street was a two-story white building with boarded-over windows, chips of paint missing from its front wall, and a heavy urine smell. There was nothing remotely attractive about the pen and I had almost decided to skip on the story, preparing myself to tell Naylor to fuck off.

I went inside, though. The entrance was down four steps and a gray door welcomed me. I played with its knob, took a deep breath and entered the establishment at my own risk. The stink of man-sweat filled my nostrils once I was inside, and my view took in the surroundings without any surprises whatsoever.

It *was* a typical gym, just as Mike had said. Weight benches were to the far right. A boxing ring sat in the center of the place. There were two wrestling mats, a number of cycles, just as many treadmills, and numerous rowers scattered here and there. A running track circled the gym's interior perimeter, climbing ropes hung down from the two-story high ceiling, and a sign painted on the wall to the far left read swimming pool & lockers, next to a narrow and dim hallway.

There were more men in the place than women, and each sported bodies from hell. It was muscleland all the way, and I felt at home.

Just as I was about to walk toward the locker room area with my gym bag and perform an hour workout, a big-boned black man the size of a dump truck made eye contact with me, smiled and confronted me. He said, "May I help you?" checking me out from head to toe, studying my ginger-colored hair, freckles on my cheeks and nose, green eyes and every pumped muscle that comprised my athletic body.

I passed him the white business card that Naylor had given me. All I could do was look at the outlined dick in his tight running shorts, which were a bright yellow. The tube of cock exposed in its breathable fabric was something of a spectacle. Like my own cock, Mr. Sampson's was plump and healthy looking. And his bare chest was just as appealing: a heaping mass of veined muscle the color of dark chocolate with hard pecs, alert nipples, and a rippled stomach that needed to be licked.

He looked at the card, nodded, checked me out again with maybe the slightest attraction and reached for my right hand to pump.

The pumping was brisk and powerful. Then he said, "You're the first hot ginger-head that has walked into this place. Welcome."

I didn't know whether to be offended or flattered, but thought it best to go with the latter. I said, "I'm Kurt Rawley, thanks for having me."

We talked for a few minutes and I learned all the details I needed to know about his establishment for my article, including that he was quite the businessman, owned two other gyms in different cities and planned on opening a fourth in the near future, as soon as this gym was up and running, and financially capable to stand on its own.

Following his mundane details he said, "Make yourself at home, Kurt."

I told him that was my intention, and the two of us separated. He walked over to a bald beefcake who was lifting over three hundred pounds and I headed for the locker room, prepared to dump my bag and begin a sweaty workout.

The locker room area was similar to others I had frequented in my bodybuilding adventures. Steam room to the right, lockers and benches to the left, showers in the rear, toilets to the far left. Nothing was unusual except for a narrow hallway next to the showers. A sign hung above its open doorway that read MR. SAMPSON'S MUSCLE PALACE.

No one was around to ask what the sign meant. So after shoving my gym bag into a locker, I decided to investigate the hallway, and whatever the gym owner's muscle palace entailed.

The hallway was long, narrow and sloped downward. I was sublevel before I realized it and in almost complete darkness. A steel door stopped my trek for the time being. The door, I assumed, led outside, probably to a trio of Dumpsters in a back alley. That wasn't the case, though.

Beyond the door was a set of six, red-illuminated underground rooms without windows or doors. Three were positioned on the right, and the other three were on the left side, forming a zigzagging pattern. Each room was different in size and content, which, after investigating, left me speechless, intrigued and quite awestruck, all at the same time.

Three hairy bears were in the first room doing a threesome circle jerk. One of them called out to me, "Come on in, guy, and help us crank these dicks."

I winked, grinned, and decided to move to the next room, which was empty.

The third room was larger than the previous two. Chains were affixed to the wall, as well as an eighteen-year-old Asian boy with a limp dick and clamps on his nipples. Some S/M fucker with a whip and leather mask was beating him. The boy loved it, asking for more.

Room number four was occupied by six young gym rats who performed an eye-catching orgy. Moans and grunts echoed within the room as the collected men acted out their top and bottom positions with great delight.

The fifth room was a huge surprise for me and I had to take a second look, just to believe that the events inside were real and not a figment of my imagination. My roommate, Mike, was there with another guy, a twink with blond hair and a cheerleader's build. Twink was on his back, sprawled over a swinging net. Mike was in the buff, ripped and beautiful, and had his cock jammed inside the little twink's tight and hairless ass. His palms were secure around the boy's ankles and kept Twink's legs open for easy access. The two rocked back and forth in hyper motion. Mike's bulbous ass was a fine piece of art as it thrust forward and then pulled away from the boy, which proved that he was fucking the beginner gym buddy with all his weight.

Sweat flung off his chiseled chest and decorated Twink's flat stomach. As Mike continued to pound the blond, creating a scene that resembled porn stars in action, Twink whimpered and begged for more ass-work.

Mike was happy to oblige, and rocked his hips into the boy's ass, pulled away and rocked into him again with Herculean power, which shifted the netting and Twink east and west.

Our eyes met for the briefest time. Mike didn't seem at all surprised to see me, and he released a palm from one of Twink's ankles and gave me a thumbs-up with an eager smile, while his center still bucked the boy on the net.

There was never a time in our three-year relationship as city roommates that I hadn't wanted to try out his skin for size, to become sexual with the jock's built frame. Unfortunately, such an occasion never transpired between us because I always thought that Mike was straight and into female cheerleaders. Had I known differently, realizing that he enjoyed a man's tight ass and close company, I would have been quite pleased to share both with him, even if I considered myself a top.

I was just about to enter the room and join the two, having every intention of banging my roommate's rear as he did Twink's, when Mr. Sampson moved up behind me in the hallway, grabbed me by my right bicep and said, "Come with me, Ginger. I have some things in mind to do to you."

I was pulled away from Mike and Twink's antics and led to the final room, which was empty except for a steel chair, lube and two latex condoms. As I was pulled into the room, I asked Mr. Sampson, "What are you going to do to me?"

I wasn't startled. Maybe I should have been, but honestly, I wasn't. Instead, I was thrilled that the black god with his firm chest and solid middle had an interest in me. How'd he know that I craved African American men, desiring their extra-large dicks and dark-colored skin? Could Mr. Sampson read my mind, or what?

He ignored my question. Rather, he faced me, drew a finger down and along my tee-covered chest and asked, "What do you think of my muscle palace?"

"Let's fuck around and then I will tell you."

He laughed.

I laughed.

And then we undressed, dropping clothes to the cement

floor, prepared to get busy with each other's flesh in a man-connected-man scene that would have left some queers blushing with utter astonishment.

Mr. Sampson sat down in the chair, toyed with the black and rigid spike at his center and said, "Lick this, Ginger."

I didn't have a problem providing men—especially dark-skinned ones—with a tour of my mouth. In fact, I often suggested such a treat; he had simply beaten me to the punch. I fell to my knees, opened my mouth and inhaled his cock as if it were a treat at a buffet.

I gagged on his shaft as it blocked my airway. Warm saliva dripped out of the corners of my mouth. Half of me believed I would drop to the floor in a state of unconsciousness because of his black cock inside my system, but I still found air to breathe through my nose.

Slurps, licks and sucking ensued on most of his chocolate-colored dick. In doing so, I strummed his balls, squeezed the hairy pair, tugged on them, and even ran a finger along the thin line of asshole between his spread thighs. I admit today, some years after this event with the black beast, that he almost suffocated me because of his inflated size. Not only did I choke on his post, but I also believed I was suffering from asphyxiation. Although I was not a master at eating cock, I felt that I had accomplished my best work with Mr. Sampson, believing that he was satisfied by my oral play because of his grumbles and occasional gasps.

Was he about to come? I thought so but wasn't sure. Perhaps this was why he said, "Stand up, Kurt, turn around and bend over."

Again, I listened like a very good boy. He bent me over in rushed motion and I felt half of his face inside my bottom. He squeezed my ass with both palms, dragged his plump tongue against my opening and became hungry behind me, licking and lapping at a hole that we both knew he was going to fuck by the end of this evening's queer blending.

One in my position would have been a little shocked to have his bottom bitten and spanked by a pump-buddy, but I wasn't in the slightest. Instead, I rather enjoyed his gnawing at my center and the swift bites to my orbs. I would be a liar if I didn't admit that he had sent me into a spin of excitement, longing for his massive dick to be plunged inside my ass instead of his tongue. Not that I was complaining, of course.

What transpired in that small room was XXX-gratifying all the way. I felt woozy in front of him, and almost lost my balance a few times because of his center-licking but caught myself at the very last second before tumbling to the hard floor. What *was* hard just happened to be the cock at my center, which bounced up and down because of his mouth and eating. At one point, because I was so elated by his irrepressible appetite, a bubble of precome leaked out of my cockhead and dribbled to the floor.

Following a string of combined minutes, he slapped my ass hard, pulled his face away from my asshole, said, "Enough," and spun me around to face him. Then his instruction was simple as he stayed seated in the steel chair: "Roll a rubber down and over my post and apply some lube to it."

I had always taken orders well as a Boy Scout while growing up in the city, and such a characteristic hadn't changed in my adulthood, since I enjoyed obeying men.

Once I was through with my task, he told me, "Back up and have a seat on me, Ginger. I want to plug your ass."

I was horny for a good fuck, particularly with Mr. Sampson and his jockish black skin. Dudes of color knew how to bang bottoms, I had learned, and I wasn't about to turn down a naughty action with the man. This is why I plummeted my compact rear onto his latex-covered mass, pushed all of my weight over the piece of meat between his legs, gasped with pain, smiled and knew that I was right in visiting his gym this evening, and his underground rooms of queer fun.

All nine of his plump and veined inches entered me with slamming speed, clear down to his balls, which were snug against my asshole and brushed the area between my thighs. As he directed his swollen bulk inside my epicenter, he dug his fingernails into my hips and moaned, "Damn, you know what you're doing."

After all of his inches were tucked inside my ass, he started banging my rear with forceful jabs. His fingertips dug into my hip, and he licked an area of my spine.

"Don't be shy," I whispered, instructing him.

"Just as I had planned," he said, and applied gentle bites to one shoulder blade, bruising my skin the way I had wanted to be bruised.

Consistent ass-jabs with his cock occurred, as well as murmurs from the man behind and underneath me. He rocketed into my rear a few times, paused, rocked into it again and pulverized my center.

Jesus wept. No, Jesus didn't have anything to do with my gym time. Instead, I wept as Mr. Sampson shoved his black dick inside me again and again and again, which caused my bottom lip to quiver with pain and delight.

"Fucking you," he said to my wall-like shoulder blades, slamming all of his muscled mass inside my rear.

I bounced my gym buddy weight up and down on his dick, and felt dizzy and confused. My breath was lost and a state of inebriated bliss discovered me. I panted for oxygen, and believed that his cock was a hand-weight being shoved up my asshole instead of his nine inches, but still I seemed to enjoy its length and width to the fullest. My ride was nothing less than rhythmic and gratifying for both of us. Quick and smooth bottom-lifts and falls occurred on his cock for numerous minutes inside the red-illuminated room, and gasps of desire filled the space, proving our lust.

How he reached around me with his left hand and jacked me off while banging my ass was spine numbing and a mystery to me since his pelvis corrupted my behind with relentless velocity. Truth was I came rather quickly on the cement floor because of such action. Five speedy hand-thrusts on my cock caused ripples of elation to spin inside my balls. Before I knew it, cream spiraled out of my nine inches and washed over the floor. White pools of the goop collected beyond our feet. I gyrated on his dick in a final north and south motion, felt tingles of euphoria sweep throughout my core and wished that my ride wasn't coming to an end.

He was just about to come, and he bucked me off his lap and told me to spin around. "Get on your knees and face me."

I listened like the good gym buddy I was and grinned from ear to ear with selfish pleasure.

Mr. Sampson cranked his nine-inch shaft a number of times, howled with excitement, ground his teeth together and drained his cock on the side of my face. A gush of white sap splatted against my right cheek, then thick cords lined my neck, and one pec. In doing so, huffing and puffing, he said to me, "Quite the load isn't it?"

I didn't object, doused in the white shit.

I was just getting ready to use a palm to remove the sticky sap from my skin when he instructed me, "Don't wipe it off, Ginger. I want to eat it up."

And he did. The African American leaned over me, extended his pink-red tongue and lapped every drop of ooze from my flesh, satisfying his own need. Dozens of tongue flicks transpired and he moaned, obviously enjoying himself.

Before I knew it, his dick-spray was removed from my skin. Every drop. Every bubble. Not a single line of residue was left, and he was exhausted, just like me.

\* \* \*

Spent, heaving for breath and perspiration covered, I said, "How do I sign up to use this gym?"

"I think you already did," Mr. Sampson said, smacking my solid ass, snapping his palm against my bottom's tight skin. Then he added, "Ginger, I rather like you. You can use Sampson's anytime you want."

Maybe he was going to be my boyfriend. Maybe not. I knew that orange and black looked pretty hot together, particularly around autumn. Until then, I had every intention of fucking him, and vice versa, mixing our sweat and bodies together with ultimate zeal.

Three seconds later my naked roommate walked into the room. Mike sported a sky-high erection, a wide grin, and pumped muscles everywhere on his body. He thwapped his dick against his abs, trotted up to me, kissed me on my lips, shoved his tongue down the back of my throat and pulled on my still-hard cock. Once he backed away from me, he demanded from Mr. Sampson and me, "I want the two of you studs to fuck me at the same time. Who's in?"

It wasn't the Mike I was used to, but I was game. The jock was always on my radar, and always would be. Now was my chance to have him, just the way I wanted him, with or without Mr. Sampson in the mix.

But Mr. Sampson was also game since he said, "Things are just getting heated up in my muscle palace tonight, guys. Let this threesome begin."

Two days later I handed my article in on time and Naylor complimented me with: "Good job. It's clean, cut and to the point, with no bullshit."

I didn't put anything in the article about Mr. Sampson's Muscle Palace. The *Herald*'s readership was far too conservative and wouldn't have been amused by such findings. Instead, I simply called the place exciting, with functional and high-tech equipment and a smiling staff.

Naylor said, "Sampson just put a sign up in front of his gym today. I saw it on my drive into the office this morning."

"What did he end up calling it?" I asked, curious.

"Sweat and Tears Gym. Nothing ordinary or spectacular. I'll add the name to your article so it reads better."

I sort of chuckled under my breath and realized that Naylor was all wrong about his comment. The gym's underground rooms called Mr. Sampson's Muscle Palace were hardly dull or like any other gym in the city. Maybe Naylor would find that out someday. Maybe not. I wasn't going to nudge my way into his life and hang out with the guy to learn something like that. Instead, I exited his office with other things on my mind, like two needy men who waited for me beneath Sweat and Tears. One was sexy and black, and the other one *supposedly* liked female cheerleaders, though I knew better. And both of them had cocks for me to ride, among other queer activities, until they erupted with fresh come, of course.

# PUMPING IVAN

### Landon Dixon

I stared at Ivan "the Terrible" Teldov, the dumbbells in my hands curling up and down on their own. The gym owner-trainer was geared up for action in a pair of tight black shorts and a tight blue muscle shirt, his chestnut-brown, rock-hard body glistening with sweat. He was looming over a guy sprawled out on a weight bench desperately trying to wrestle a loaded barbell off his chest, urging the groaning man on in his subtle, profanity-laden, 120-decibel way.

Ivan leaned in even closer, big hands on big, bunched quads, square-jawed face inches away from the other man's tear-streaked one. He screamed at the guy to push out that final excruciating rep, spit spraying out of his snarling mouth.

My cock was the hardest appendage on my underdeveloped 180-pound, eighteen-year-old body as I watched, bulging the mesh in my shorts. I was pumping iron, wishing I was pumping buzz-cut blond muscle-stud Ivan instead.

Just before closing time, it was my turn to get the Ivan the Terrible training experience.

"Round 'em out at the top!" the big man barked, the gym empty now. "Like you're bear-huggin' someone!"

I clumped the dumbbells together over my head, hurriedly banging out another set of chest flies, hopefully to Ivan's satisfaction. The man's dimple-chinned face, bulging bronze body and drill sergeant intensity were more than a little intimidating up close, even after two weeks of getting yelled at.

"You wanna feel it right here," he growled, reaching down and prodding my chest through my T-shirt. His warm, blunt fingertip ran along the swollen edge of one of my pecs, brushing over a nipple.

I shivered, the dumbbells jumping in my hands. I barely had the strength to bring them back together overhead to complete the set.

"What's next?" Ivan demanded.

I scrambled upright on the bench. "Uh, like your plan says, I was, um, just going to do some sit-ups to finish off my workout."

"Quittin' already?"

"I've been here two hours!"

He snorted, and tousled my curly mop of brown hair. "Crunch time then, junior."

The man of striated granite was actually only a few years older than me, but you'd never know it from the way he handled himself, and others. I lay back down on the bench and brought my feet up. He grabbed my knees, shoved my legs closer. "Go!" he yelled.

I interlaced my fingers behind my head quicker than a perp on *Cops*. I started crunching abs. Ivan grabbed the back of my head and pushed me higher, bumping my elbows into my knees.

"You wanna feel it right along here," he snarled, letting go of my throbbing neck and yanking my tee up, poking my stomach.

I churned up and down like a madman, cock swelling along with my abs as Ivan traced my ribbed stomach with his fingertip. And when that thick finger trailed all the way down to my shorts, bulged the waistband and squirmed inside, I almost did a face-plant into my knees.

"You're gettin' a nice little six-pack, kid," he said, before snapping my shorts and turning and striding away.

I flew through fifty reps like nothing, then floated out of the gym, headed for the locker room, the warm memory of Ivan's soft fingertip still tickling my abs, teasing even lower, filling my pumped-up body and groin. Until my dizzy brain suddenly registered the grunting and groaning of another type of workout going on, in the steam room.

I peeked into the sauna through a partially fogged-up window, and my cock flexed even harder. Two musclemen were putting in the most intimate of hot, hard-male exercise sessions, one guy giving his buddy the iron bar from behind.

The black-haired dude was bent in half, clinging to an upper tier wooden bench, the blond hunk pounding cock into his ass, hard and fast, their built, bronze bodies gleaming under the muted lights, in the mist. I'd seen the pair around the gym before—Glen and Brendan—but never working out this passionately before. Glen's hips were flying, muscled buttocks clenching and unclenching, cock pistoning, hammering Brendan's sweet ass, rocking the moaning man almost loose from his perch.

I quickly grabbed on to my hardened dick through my satin shorts and started rubbing, getting an eye- and handful. Brendan was screaming, "Fuck me! Fuck me!" Which was exactly what Glen was doing, head flung back and muscles surging, chiseled body splashing against rippling ass in the billowing steam.

I yanked my shorts down and cock out, getting skin on skin, fisting my raging member in rhythm with Glen's frantic thrusting. Until Brendan smacked the wooden bench with his hand, tapping out, and the guys hastily switched positions. Glen ended up hunched up on his back in the first row, anxiously pulling on his big, cut cock, Brendan clutching the guy's legs against his shredded body while he worked his own stiff prong up Glen's gaping asshole.

I went back to applauding the men's steamy exhibition with my hand on my cock, stroking even faster, as Brendan plugged into his hard-bodied lover. Glen groaned, tugging on his nipples, his cock, his blown-up, pec-plated chest heaving as Brendan hit bottom.

Brendan gripped his buddy's ankles and churned his hips, brutally cocking the blond, stretching out the man's chute with the hottest of warm-up exercises. "Split me in two, fucker!" Glen hollered, pressing his balls down and heavy-stroking his prick.

I pumped my cock as Brendan pumped Glen, fantasizing even as I stared at the dripping muscle-studs that I was pumping Ivan. I had the hardcore trainer laid out on the end of the slippery steam bench, pounding reps into his hot, tight manhole, anally drilling him like he'd verbally drilled me so many times. My trim, toned body bounced off his smooth, mounded buttcheeks, cock plowing his superheated vise of an ass. He screamed at me to tear him a new one, sausage fingers viciously twisting his fat nipples, ham fist urgently jacking his engorged cock.

And just when Brendan shouted out his ecstasy, thick muscles locking up and down his glistening body and tendons screaming, and sprayed hot cum into Glen's bowels, as Glen jerked ropes of the salty white stuff out of his own jumping cock; just when my own balls boiled up to the critical point and my dong went super-hard in prelude to unloading its joy, flooding my imaginary Ivan with my love; that's when the gym door suddenly whooshed open.

I stuffed my shorts full of cock and hustled my ass on into the locker room. I didn't want anyone spying on me, after all.

I stripped off my workout gear and went into the shower room, got the hot water going, building up some new steam, soaping

my tight, blood-pumped body. I had the communal six-head
shower facility all to myself, so I quickly got the dirty work out
of the way—cleaning myself off. Then I got down and dirty,
grabbing on to my quivering erection with my hand and the
bar of soap and stroking again, dreaming again, the hot water
washing over my stoked body in erotic waves.

The suds surged around my swollen prick, and I was engulfed
by even more heat. I closed my eyes and took water in the face,
urgently rubbing my cock, squeezing my nipples, fantasizing
about Ivan's finger trailing down into my fur, moving slowly,
lightly, exquisitely along the hard, pulsing length of my cock.
I torqued up the pressure on my dick as Ivan the Terrible deli-
cately swirled his finger around my bloated hood, brushing the
supersensitive underside where shaft met head.

"You're the last one here!" someone yelled.

My eyes snapped open and the bar of soap squirted out of
my hand, and went racing along the tile floor. Ivan was striding
toward me, completely and utterly and breathtakingly naked,
muscles-on-muscles body blazing a sun-kissed brown. His cock
bobbed in between his thick, muscle-cut legs, heavy balls and
the surrounding area as hairless as the rest of him. I crowded
the wall, desperately trying to hide my excitement, and embarrassment.

He came right up next to me and twisted some taps around,
spraying water over his ripped body—beautiful. "Feels good
after a tough workout, huh?" he said, tilting his head back,
water splashing off his pec-cleaved chest.

"Yeah...good," I mumbled. My cockhead was kissing the
slick, tiled wall, dick refusing to go down.

"You've made a lotta progress in only a coupla weeks," he
stated, glancing my way as I glanced away. "You're even pumpin'
in the shower now, huh?" He laughed.

I didn't know what to say or do. But Ivan knew what he was

doing. He slapped my ass, hard, the sharp, wet contact echoing like a gunshot. My butt stung and my body surged.

The hard man put a heavy hand on my bare shoulder and gently turned me around, staring at my pointing, twitching cock, a warm, wonderful smile creasing his full, red lips. My balls went tighter than the guy's ass and a shiver ran through me.

"This muscle's sure well developed," Ivan said softly, reaching out and encircling my throbbing shaft with his fingers, making me jump. "But it still needs regular exercise, right?"

"R-right," I garbled, a wild tingling sensation shimmering all through my body as Ivan squeezed my cock. I gasped for air, got water, the man's warm, soft palm sliding up and down my shaft.

He stroked and stroked me, leisurely, wickedly, my head spinning like the water down the drain. Then he tilted my pole up and pressed it against my body, pressed his body against mine, his cock into my cock. He took me in his arms and kissed me. I gleefully threw my arms around the hunk, our hot, slippery bodies melting together, muscles fusing, his soft, wet lips pressing against my lips.

He kissed me harder and deeper, devouring me as I felt up his rugged back. He swam his tongue into my open mouth and bumped it into my tongue. He explored the inside of my mouth with his hungry, twisting tongue, choking me, painting my trembling lips. I tried to fight back with my tongue, but I was too weak in the face of his erotic onslaught, his powerful grip, my body burning and my brain gone fuzzy. All I could do was feebly move my hips, grind my meat against his meat, secure in the iron man's iron grip.

Mouth still working over my mouth, Ivan drifted his huge hands down my back and onto my bum, gripping and squeezing my pale, trembling buttcheeks. I moaned into his mouth, and he lifted me right up off the water-washed floor, savagely kneading my buttocks, my cock sliding sensuously over his chiseled abs.

Finally, he broke away from my mouth, and let me breathe again. I opened my eyes and stared at the man, his strong hands working my ass flesh to the point of pleasurable pain, our cocks squeezing together again. My eyes and mind suddenly cleared and my body brimmed with sexual energy. I grabbed on to the stud's chest, digging my fingers into the meat of his pecs, pinching his creamed-coffee nipples between my fingers. His eyelids fluttered and he groaned, and I gained even more strength from his loss of control.

I rubbed his streaming chest, and rolled his swollen buds, his armored body shuddering against me. I increased the pressure on his nipples, and he looked down at me, blue eyes gone misty. I stuck out my tongue and tickled a rigid jutter, and he jerked, fingernails biting into my bum. "Yeah, suck my nipples!" he moaned.

I swirled my pink tongue around the first tan, pebbly nipple and then the other, tasting the man, teasing him, watching and feeling his nipples stiffen. I sealed my moist lips around a fully blossomed bud and sucked on it, gazing up into Ivan's eyes. He bit his lip and plied my ass, overblown body trembling as I tugged at his nipple.

I bounced my head back and forth between his clenched pecs, licking and sucking his nipples. He grunted, "Fuck!" when I sank my teeth into one of his buds.

Then he grabbed my head and pulled me up, mashing his mouth against mine again. I fought with his thrashing tongue this time, our slippery tongues entwining over and over, until he shoved me back and dropped to his knees, squatting in front of my dripping dong.

"You sure are built," the behemoth marveled at my feet, hot breath steaming against my cock. He gripped me at the base with one hand, and cupped my balls with the other, nipping at my mushroomed hood with his ultra-white teeth. Then he took me in his mouth and sucked on my cockhead.

"Jesus!" I yelped.

Ivan pulled on my hood with his lips, fingering my tightened ball sac, and pumping my pulsating shaft. He cushioned the underside of my dick with his tongue then wagged his tongue back and forth, and I went weak in the knees.

The big man pushed his head forward, my long, hard cock sliding easily in between his lips, down into the wet-hot depths of his cauldron of a mouth. I flung my head back and moaned, clutching at his buzz cut and shaking with delight. He sucked my cock, wet lips sliding back and forth on my shaft, taking me down almost to the roots and then back up again, never letting up on the pressure in either direction, pumping me with his mouth like he taught the men in his gym to pump the iron.

I churned my hips, fucking the guy's mouth as he wet-vacuumed my cock. I thrust faster, and he sucked harder, my balls tingling almost past the control point. He sensed it and jerked his head back, leaving me dangling.

"You're gonna pump my ass, big boy," he declared, squeezing my cock, and licking precum from my slit.

He stood up, and I got a good look at his prick. It was hard and high, but disproportionately small compared to the rest of his mammoth body. Then he turned his back on me and flattened his hands up against the wall, bending at the waist, showing me his bronzed, brick-hard ass. "Fuck my ass!" he hissed over his shoulder, thrusting out his cheeks.

I quickly re-soaped my cock with a quivering hand, reaching out and caressing the man's heavy, round buttocks. Then I sudsed up his crack. He jerked when my fingers probed in between his water-pebbled mounds. Jerked again when I pulled out my fingers and plugged in my cap. I found his opening, gripped his hips and pushed forward, plunging inside of him. He shoved backward, his ass swallowing me whole.

"Jesus!" I groaned, the heated, velvet tightness unbelievable.

The temperature in that sexual sauna went nuclear as I started moving my hips, slipped, then got a good fucking rhythm going, churning Ivan's gripping chute. He clawed at the wall, head and back arched, thunder cheeks rippling as I smacked up against them, banging his ass.

I held on to his hips and on for the ride, blinking steam and perspiration out of my eyes, pistoning rock-hard cock up the guy's butt. I went faster and faster, oiling back and forth in that vise-like chute, stretching him out and pounding him down.

He desperately grabbed on to his flapping cock and fisted. I wildly slammed him over and over, the hot, wet smack of flesh against flesh filling my ears, the wicked pressure on my pumping cock filling my body with molten eroticism. My balls boiled out of control.

"Fuck, I'm comin'!" Ivan cried just ahead of me. He was on his tiptoes, his big bad body dancing around on the end of my driving dick as he jacked streams of semen out of his ruptured cock.

My senses went into overload as I went on savagely spanking the guy's shivering bum with my thrusting body, plunging cock exploding deep in his beautiful ass. I was jolted by ecstasy, blasting sizzling jizz into my man's sexual core. I came what felt like forever, with a terrible intensity that matched even Ivan's.

My big, tough muscleman works me hard in the gym, and I work him hard in the whirlpool, and the sauna, and the shower room, pumping iron and then pumping Ivan. I'm getting stronger every day.

# WORKING OUT THE KINKS

## Katya Harris

Come on. Last set. Give me twenty more."

Muscles straining, Cam did another pull-up. "Shut the fuck up, Trey," he hissed through gritted teeth. His arms felt like jelly, his whole body a throbbing ache after his intense workout. He didn't think he could do one more, let alone another nineteen. All he wanted to do was crawl into the corner of his gym, and die.

Standing close by, Trey grinned up at him. "Ah, don't be a pussy. Nineteen more. Chop-chop."

Cam grunted with the effort of doing another. Sweat poured from his body, tickling his skin as it trickled down his arms and bare chest. He distracted himself from the pain screaming through his body by imagining punching Trey in his smirking face.

"Stop picturing yourself hitting me."

"How do you always know?" Cam puffed out each word as he lowered himself back down in one smooth, controlled movement.

Leaning against the mirror-covered wall behind him, his arms crossed over the impressively muscled expanse of his chest, Trey told him, "You get this look on your face."

"What look?" Cam lifted his chin over the bar and back down again.

"A decidedly violent one." Trey licked his lips. "You look like you want to do some very bad things to me."

A frisson of sensation sizzled through Cam. It nearly made him let go of the bar. Firming his grip, he did another pull-up. "Fuck off, Trey."

"Oh," Trey taunted, "Someone's feeling like a tough guy today."

"I feel like a tough guy everyday." The retort slipped out of Cam's mouth and he instantly regretted it. In the mirror he could see the stripe of red that decorated his cheeks and blushed even more.

Trey laughed, a deep rumbling chuckle. "I just bet you do. Do your girlfriends know about that?"

His voice was amused as he asked the question, but Cam would have to be a real idiot not to hear the bite snapping at the end of each word.

He did two more pull-ups before answering. "Is that why you're punishing me? Because I took that model to the premiere?"

Trey snorted. "I don't think there's a worse punishment than being in that dumb bitch's company, and I'm not punishing you. I'm getting your scrawny ass in shape. It'll be hard to do all those stunts with your current weedy status."

Anger powered Cam through another pull-up. "I'm not weedy and Macy isn't dumb."

"But she is a bitch."

Cam couldn't really deny it. Macy Sinclair was the most self-centered, egotistical person he had ever met. A singer turned actress, she had simpered prettily on his arm as the paparazzi snapped their pictures, but she had looked at him as if he were a piece of shit scraped off her Jimmy Choo's the rest of the time. His agent, who had set them up to begin with, might assure him that she was an up-and-coming commodity, and that being seen with her would boost his profile ahead of a big audition he had coming up, but he wouldn't be caught dead with her again.

He wasn't going to tell Trey that though.

If Cam could have shrugged he would have. "It was fun." A total lie; he had spent most of the night gritting his teeth to keep from telling her where to go. "What? Are you jealous?"

Another pull-up made eight. Only twelve more to go.

Trey's eyes narrowed. "Hardly." Pushing off the glass, he stalked over to him. Cam refused to stop, keeping his eyes fixed on his reflection rather than dipping down to meet Trey's.

Nine.

Ten.

The lick of a hot tongue on his belly made Cam jerk.

Cam glared down at the other man. "What the hell, Trey? You nearly made me fall."

Trey grinned up at him, blue eyes dancing like a sunlit summer sky. "You weren't paying attention to me."

"You're my personal trainer," Cam reminded him. "You're meant to be paying attention to me."

Trey's breath feathered over the sweat-slick skin of his stomach. Little tickles of sensation shivered through Cam's nerves.

"Stop it," he grunted as he did number eleven.

"I'm not doing anything."

"Bullshit," he declared and then gasped. His arms felt like they were going to pull out of their sockets.

"Come on, Cam." He was so close to him, his lips brushed against the taut muscles of his client's abdomen. "Nine more."

Cam chuffed with effort, but he couldn't make it to twelve. Hanging there, he shook his head. "I can't do it."

"Yes, you can." At their current positions, Trey's head was just below his chest. His head tilting back, he grinned at him, mischief twinkling in his eyes. "Nine more and I'll suck your cock."

Heat blasted along Cam's veins, racing toward his groin. "Fuck."

Trey chuckled. "We can do that too."

Groaning, Cam managed number twelve and then thirteen, barely. "Stop trying to bribe me."

"I'm your personal trainer, Cam." Now it was his turn to remind him. "It's my job, isn't it, to motivate you?"

Cam grunted. His arms shook as he wobbled his way to fourteen, fifteen. "Trey, I don't know what to tell you, but I don't think other trainers offer their clients sexual services for them to finish their sessions."

Trey winked. "How would you know?"

Cam had tried to make Trey jealous, but now he felt the sting. It got him through numbers sixteen, seventeen and eighteen.

"Fuck you, Trey."

"Soon enough," he quipped. "That's it, Cam. Just two more and then I'll suck that big dick of yours. It looks like it needs a workout of its own."

Gritting his teeth, Cam growled his way through his nineteenth pull-up.

"Yeah, that's it. One more. You can do it."

Blood, hot as lava, filled Cam's muscles as he forced them to do the last pull-up. The sound that tore from his throat was animalistic, a furious rumble, as the veins in his forehead popped and sweat streamed from every pore. His body hated him, but he did it, his chin lifting over the bar. Carefully lowering himself down, he let go of the bar and dropped to his feet. Relief was better than drugs. He exhaled a satisfied breath and then inhaled a shocked one as Trey dropped to his knees in front of him, his hands pulling down the waistband of his workout shorts.

"Trey! What the fuck?"

Hunger sharpened Trey's features as he glanced up at him. "I told you I'd suck your cock if you did it. Well, you did it."

Cam's shorts puddled around his feet and left him naked. No longer confined, his cock sprang forward, eager for some attention. "I have to cool down," Cam reminded him weakly. Fuck, he was horny and he couldn't take his eyes off their reflection. Trey, half-dressed with his densely muscled back on display, kneeling in front of his own naked, sweat-soaked and flushed body. No matter how many times Cam saw them like this the sight was just as powerful. Lust mingled with the adrenaline in his system, a potent cocktail that went to his head like neat whiskey. Fuck, but he wanted him bad.

Wrapping one hand around the base of Cam's erection, Trey angled it forward. Opening his mouth, he delivered a slow lick to the weeping head of Cam's cock. His eyes fluttered shut. "Damn, you taste good." Opening his eyes, he pursed his lips and blew a soft breath across the damp crown, smiling as Cam groaned. "We'll work out your kinks like this."

Cam's hands slid into Trey's messy brown hair, clenched around the silky strands. "Yes," he hissed. "Do it."

Cam couldn't see him, but he knew Trey was smiling. "You're the boss."

Cam shuddered as Trey sucked the head of his cock into his hot mouth. His tongue played along its flared edge, teased the sweet spot underneath.

Cam's hands pulled Trey's hair tight. "Don't tease," he told him. "Suck me."

Trey backed off, his mouth coming free of Cam's cock with a soft pop. "Not yet. You're always in too much of a hurry. You need to slow down." Licking down the length of Cam's erection, he came to his balls. The perfectly smooth, shaved globes were tight with Cam's arousal. Trey nuzzled his face against them, kissing and licking.

Cam's breath hitched. "Fuck, that feels amazing."

"See." Trey's voice was muffled as he burrowed his face farther between Cam's spread thighs. His tongue flickered over the sensitive area behind Cam's balls. His free hand curved around Cam, grasping his asscheek roughly.

Widening his stance, Cam tilted his hips, cursing again as the tip of Trey's tongue flickered over his anus. "Trey," he moaned. He didn't know whether it was in complaint or encouragement. Heat rushed over him, scorching him to the bone. "Oh god."

His trainer made a hungry noise and then he was licking his way back up Cam's cock. His head dipped and he swallowed it down, the muscles of his throat rippling and massaging. Cam shook beneath their onslaught. His hips bumped forward, his groin meeting Trey's face with each stroke. His fingers dug into the other man's scalp, holding his bobbing head still as he fucked his face. Cam always worried about hurting him when they did this, but over his own hectic breathing, he could hear the hungry, almost delirious moans Trey made as he took him.

"Fuck, Trey. I'm gonna come." Cam could feel it, sensation at the base of his spine like a million tiny lightning strikes, his spunk boiling up his shaft. He tried to pull away, to stop. He didn't want to come yet; he wanted this to go on forever.

Trey's hands clamped on to the flexing muscles of Cam's ass, pulling him forward. His sucking increased, his throat massaging Cam's dick insistently every time he swallowed around the swollen head.

Orgasm slammed into Cam. His body shot rigid, his hips

thrusting recklessly forward to bury his cock as deep in Trey's throat as possible. Words fell in an incoherent stream from Cam's slack lips, the pleasure of his cum pulsing from his dick wiping all thought away.

When sense finally returned to him, he shuddered with pleasurable aftershocks as Trey slid off his still semihard dick. The other man's lips were red and swollen, and when he spoke his voice was even rougher than usual. "Enjoy that, did you?"

Cam blushed. "You know I did." Cupping Trey's jaw, he brushed his thumb against his abused mouth. "I'm sorry."

"I'm not."

Cam cried out as Trey pulled at him with rough hands. Still weak-kneed from orgasm, it wasn't hard for Trey to tumble him to the ground.

Twisting to land on his back, Cam stared wide-eyed as Trey crawled over him. The other man's mouth slanted over his and Cam's eyes fluttered shut, a moan pouring from his mouth into Trey's. Fuck, was there anything sexier than tasting his cum in Trey's mouth? The only thing he could think of was actually fucking him.

Eagerly, he licked the taste of himself from Trey's lips, ferreted out every hint of him from the cavern of his mouth. Trey flattened his body over his, pressing him into the floor that was only a fraction harder than he was. Trey's cock dug sharply into his belly and Cam slid his hands down the slick planes of Trey's back to his ass. Grabbing hold, he rocked the other man against him, loving the hard pressure of the other man's cock digging into his hip. He loved it so much, his own dick started to surge back to insatiable life despite the mind-scrambling orgasm he'd just had. Christ, that only ever happened with Trey.

"Fuck me."

Trey smiled down at him. "What's the magic word?"

"Now."

Cam yelped as Trey nipped sharply at his bottom lip.

"The magic word."

Cam sucked in a breath, the spot on his lip throbbing in time with his pounding heart. "Please," he whispered.

Trey nibbled along the line of his jaw. "Mmm, not enough. Tell me what you want." His voice was a dark, syrupy whisper in Cam's ear.

Lust ignited Cam's blood. Pinned beneath Trey's weight, he squirmed but not to get away. "Please, Trey," he whimpered. "Please fuck me."

"More," Trey demanded.

"Oh god, put your dick in me," Cam nearly screamed. "Please."

"All you had to do was ask."

Getting on his knees, Trey rolled up onto his feet. The bulge of his erection was a thick hump behind the skintight shorts he favored. He palmed it, rubbing its length before his hands went to his waistband. "Get on your knees. Face the mirror."

Excitement fizzed in Cam's blood. Chest heaving with his rapid breaths, he rolled over and lifted himself onto all fours. All the pain and exertion of his workout had vanished. The only agony he felt now was the desperate need to feel Trey filling his body.

Spreading his knees wide, his hips canted up and his spine arching, he stared at the wanton picture he made in the mirror. Behind him, Trey stared down at his spread ass, his face stark in its lust as he stroked his cock through the thin material of his shorts.

"Beautiful."

Cam blushed like a girl.

Getting to his feet and walking over to a table by the door, Trey rummaged through a drawer. Cam watched him, his body quaking as he walked back with a tube in his hand. He had to remind himself to breathe when Trey dropped to his knees behind him.

The lube, when Trey squeezed some onto his asshole, was shockingly cold. Cam gasped and then groaned as Trey massaged it into the flexing hole with his finger. He tried to push back, to make that finger slip inside him; he knew it would, so easily, just like he knew it would feel so wickedly good. Trey stopped him, his free hand spread wide on Cam's ass and holding him still.

"A-a-ahh," he admonished. "Not yet, you greedy thing."

No wonder Cam often thought about hitting him, not that he ever would. The world might not know it, not yet, but he loved him.

Trey's thick finger screwed into his butt. Cam groaned, his fingers clawing at the mat beneath him.

"There, is that better?"

Cam's neck arched, little zips of electricity streaking up his spine. "Yes," he hissed.

In and out, Trey's finger was slowly driving him crazy. "Please." He couldn't wait, didn't want to.

"Another one then."

A second thick digit joined the first one, stretching Cam open. His cock was so hard again it was digging into his stomach, precum smearing his belly.

"What about another?" Trey asked him, lust humming in his rough voice. "Can you take it?"

Cam would and could take anything Trey dished out to him. "Oh god, yes."

Three fingers crammed in his ass. Cam yelled out, the harsh sound echoing in the room.

"Aren't you glad you have your own gym?" Trey taunted him, his fingers flexing and scissoring in the tight clasp of Cam's bumhole. "There's nothing like a post-workout fucking, is there?"

Cam barely heard what the other man said, and he didn't care. The only thing he could concentrate on was the packed-full feeling in his rectum, the need to come again beating at his brain. Dropping his upper body so that his shoulders rested on the mat, he reached down with one hand and fisted his aching dick. Teeth bit down on the curve of his raised ass and he nearly came then and there, the little bit of pain making the pleasure burn all the hotter.

"Naughty boy," Trey breathed across his ass before he licked the throbbing spot. Still pumping his fingers in and out, he reached round with his other hand, placing it over Cam's as he jacked himself. "God, you're sexy."

"Then fuck me."

Trey's hands slipped away and Cam couldn't hold back his moan.

"If you want me to fuck you, show me how much you want me," Trey demanded softly. "Me and no one else."

Knowing what he wanted, Cam reached behind him. His hands grasped his own asscheeks, pulling them apart to expose the pucker of his anus. "I want you, Trey. Just you."

The growl that came from behind him sent a visceral thrill racing up Cam's spine. He closed his eyes, savoring the feel of the blunt head of Trey's cock pressing against his asshole. He bit his lip as his anus started to give, tremors shaking him as his body slowly accepted the thick intrusion of Trey's dick. Sweat broke out over his skin in a feverish rush. Even preparing him with three fingers wasn't enough for Trey to enter him easily. He was just too damn big. The taste of blood filled Cam's mouth as his lip gave beneath the pressure of his teeth. It wasn't pleasure that filled him with Trey's cock; it was pure fucking ecstasy.

Trey's big hands smoothed over his back and ass. "That's it, baby, just a little bit more."

Desperation raked jagged claws down Cam's body. "I want you in me. Now. Please."

Trey's hips snapped forward, his dick buried to the hilt. Pressed up against Cam's butt, he ground himself into him. "Is that what you want?"

Gasping, barely able to breathe, Cam choked out, "Yes."

Anchoring his hands on Cam's hips, Trey pulled back and thrust forward. Once. Twice. The third time, he stayed deep. "Look up, baby. I want you to watch me fuck you. I want you to see what you do to me."

Cam did as he was told. Resting his chin on the floor, his arms stretched out and braced in front of him, he watched as Trey fucked him. His teeth clattered with the force of Trey's thrusts. Their flesh slapped together as loud as thunder, each clap followed by a blast of pleasure as their balls crashed together.

Cam couldn't look away as Trey shafted into him. The perfectly defined planes of his chest and stomach, the heavy muscles roping his arms, flexed in a symphony of motion as Trey powered into him. It was the look on Trey's face though, that made Cam hurtle toward orgasm. There was lust there, pleasure and rapture, but there was also love.

It was too much and Cam only had a moment to yell out, "I'm coming," before his cum was spurting from him in long hot ribbons that decorated his chest and stomach.

His ass squeezed down on Trey's shuttling cock. Trey roared, his head tilting back to the ceiling as he slammed his hips forward at the same time he pulled Cam's hips back. Another spasm of pleasure ripped through Cam, tearing a scream from his throat, and then another as Trey filled his ass with his searing hot cum.

Falling forward, Trey blanketed his body with his larger one. Sweat slicked them both.

"I think that's your workout for the day," he gasped in Cam's ear.

A huff of laughter burst from Cam's lips. "I love you, you fucking asshole."

Trey nuzzled a kiss on his neck. "I love you too."

# SAFARI

## Sasha Payne

Going to the gym with Ken was like being taken to Santa's workshop and not being allowed to touch any of the toys. Everywhere Angel looked he could see half-naked men: some of them were bulging with muscles, some of them were trim and some of them were positively bearish. Most of them were hot. All of them he'd do except Ken. Angel glanced at his trainer; the older man was glaring at a couple of bodybuilders wandering through on their way to the weight room. Ken always derided them as "meatheads," but Angel didn't care about the meat in their heads. Not the head that Ken meant, anyway.

"I hope that lunatic isn't here," Ken muttered. "He'd eat you alive."

Angel grinned. Dan Lyon was the gym's *bête noire*, a man whose name was whispered in the showers with a mix of fear and desire. Angel had yet to meet him. Ken went out of his way to avoid training during Lyon's gym days, but in the run-up to the semifinals Angel's gym time was being ramped up. Surely he'd run into the gym's alpha dog sooner or later? Angel wondered what Lyon looked like. Would he be obviously domineering at first sight? Would he be seductive? Lyon's victims were notoriously unwilling to discuss their very public ravishment, yet nobody left the gym. Nobody called the cops. Nobody even complained to management.

Angel wondered if Lyon would consider him worthy prey. With so much choice would he even attract the attention of the gym's notorious predator?

"Come on, we haven't got all day," Ken snapped.

Angel sighed. With Ken fussing around the chances of his becoming anyone's conquest seemed dim.

There was a haze of heat in the weight room. The room was full of men, muscular men pushing their bodies hard. Everywhere Dan Lyon looked, he saw muscular, hard bodies gleaming with sweat. There was no chitchat. Just grunts and heavy breathing. The sounds of a heavy workout. The sounds of sex. The breathing got heavier as Dan prowled past men who didn't know if they should sigh or exhale in relief. Dan was still young, only twenty-three, but he had been the big dog for a long time. He loved that his name was both a wish and a warning. It didn't matter how you felt about him before he chose you. It didn't matter if you hated him or worshipped him. He took whomever he wanted, and they were grateful. Pathetically grateful.

Dan was only a little over average height, but people always remembered him as taller, as broader. He had shoulder-length fair hair that fell in a mass of thick, loose curls. His tanned skin shone with a thin layer of oil. Dan didn't come to the gym just to lift weights, and he always liked to be ready for anything.

There was a small, slim man using Dan's favorite bench set. None of the regulars would've touched it on a bet. The man was older than Dan. Late forties. There were slips of gray in his black hair and tiny, fine lines at the corner of his eyes. Nothing special but nothing awful either. The spotter was shorter, stockier and with cropped gray hair. He was better looking but still nothing too amazing. Really, if they weren't in his way he wouldn't bother with them. They were wearing matching sweats. Dan almost rolled his eyes. Cozy couples. They should've been at one of those boutique gyms—the sort with a spa and a steam room. The sort for people playing at getting fit. They thought it was funny probably. Being here with the regular folks. Like being on safari. Well, they were going to realize the animals weren't all toothless.

Dan watched the man at the weights realize he was the center of much nervous attention. The spotter didn't. The would-be bodybuilder put the equipment back in position and licked his lips.

"Can I help you?" His voice quivered a little.

Dan jerked his thumb and the man sat up quickly.

"Chad!" the spotter said.

Dan saw that there was more anxiety than confidence in his eyes. Andrew was the sort whose nervousness made him aggressive.

"It's okay, Andrew," Chad said, sitting up.

"It isn't! What do you want?" Andrew demanded, glaring at Dan.

Dan sighed. From the other machines someone sniggered. Dan didn't bother to look; he knew they weren't sniggering at him.

He stepped forward into Andrew's personal space. Andrew's shoulders stiffened but his Adam's apple bobbed frantically.

"I want your boy off my equipment," Dan said.

"I'm off! I'm off! I don't want any trouble!"

"I'm not frightened of some little gym bully," Andrew sneered.

Dan took another step closer. This time Andrew stepped

back, involuntarily. Two more steps forward. Two more steps back. Dan saw Andrew realize that he'd backed himself into a wall. Andrew swallowed as Dan planted a hand on the wall and leaned over him.

"Get down on your knees and suck me off," Dan said.

Andrew looked over at Chad, who simply shrugged.

"What if I say no?"

"I'm not threatening you, Andrew. Just saying what's going to happen. You're going to suck me off. Then Chad is going to lie down on the exercise bench and I'm going to fuck him while you watch. While everyone watches."

Andrew looked in Dan's placid, unyielding eyes and sank down to his knees. There was some shuffling as the silent audience sought a better view. Dan didn't look at them, just at the slim, sinewy man knelt in front of him. He smiled as Andrew tugged down Dan's shorts over the massive, slab-like thighs and stared. It wasn't a new reaction. Dan was proud of his body but his cock was his pride: ten inches long, and almost as thick as his wrist. Dan was cut and the purple head glistened in the flickering fluorescent light.

Dan put a hand on Andrew's head and pushed him face-down, feeling Andrew flinch. Dan could tell that Andrew fancied himself the daddy in his relationship with Chad, which only made doing this all the more fun. Dan put both hands on his head, holding it in place. As Andrew opened his mouth, Dan tilted his head up so that their eyes met.

"Relax your throat," Dan said, "I like it deep."

"Doesn't do it much," Chad muttered.

Dan laughed and Andrew almost spluttered in protest, wanting to object but gagged by the girth of Dan's cock.

"The practice will do him good, then," Dan said. He felt Andrew grip his hips for balance. He filled Andrew's mouth with his cock, until Andrew had to force his jaw wider to roll his tongue around and suck. Dan rolled his eyes. Andrew was enthusiastic but needed practice. He could see Andrew was distracted too, very aware of their audience, and of Chad watching as he was forcefully fucked in the mouth. Andrew needed some lessons in concentration as well as technique.

Dan winked at Andrew, smiled at his confusion, and then pulled his head forward. Instead of thrusting, the younger man was moving Andrew's head, using his face like some disposable sex toy. You're nothing, the wink said. I'm going to do this and there's nothing you can do about it. You can't even argue as I use you, as I fuck your face harder, faster and deeper. You might cough, you might struggle with my huge dick as it fills your mouth and throat, and I won't stop, because I don't care. Worse than all that, as I humiliate you in front of your lover and dozens of men you don't know, as I turn you into a receptacle for my spunk, you'll enjoy it. And I'll know you do.

Dan's grip tightened and he felt Andrew tense. He was close to coming. His fingers were wound tightly into Andrew's hair and he thrust faster and deeper into Andrew's mouth. Dan came and his come filled Andrew's mouth. He was vaguely aware of Andrew attempting to shift back, to slip Dan's flaccid member from his mouth, but Dan automatically held him in place. After a couple of seconds, Dan let out a breath and opened his eyes. He looked down at Andrew, who signaled frantically to be released. Dan just raised his eyebrows, and Andrew sagged, his message received and understood. He opened his throat and swallowed the thick, salty fluid.

Ken folded his arms as he watched Angel practicing on the horizontal bar. It was only getting worse: the more he saw his student, the more he wanted him. Angel was nineteen. Old enough, but sleeping with him would be an appalling breach of trust which would ruin Ken's reputation. Besides,

Angel had already turned him down. That stung, especially as he made eyes at everyone else in pants. The only thing between Angel and complete whoredom was opportunity, not intent. It didn't help that his appearance matched his name. He looked as though butter wouldn't melt in his mouth. It didn't take much batting of those huge innocent-seeming eyes to make a man think he was about to deflower some tender little virgin. Ken could see a few now, watching Angel on the bar. If the boy made it to the Olympics he'd be too exhausted to compete.

Ken tore his eyes away from Angel and glared around the room. He had a nagging feeling of being watched and he'd heard too many stories of what went on in the weight room to ignore the sensation.

Instead of the hulking meathead he was expecting, he saw a cute blond twink. Ken tried a smile, and got a grade-A come-hither look in return. The twink sauntered away toward the locker room. He glanced back at Ken over his shoulder, and smirked invitingly. Ken hesitated for a moment, saw that Angel was engrossed on the bars, and then followed the twink.

"What's your name?" he asked as they slipped into the storage room.

The twink gave him a look.

"No names," Ken said, "Right." He unbuckled his belt and drew it from his pants.

"Here." The twink slid his fingers into the loops of Ken's pants and pulled him closer. "No names. No small talk. No personal stuff. Just two men, fucking. We good?"

"We're good."

Ken took a better look at the young man opposite. He was young, handsome, and arrogant as hell. It wasn't original and it sure as hell wasn't rare. Had he ever been that arrogant? He was never that handsome.

The twink unbuttoned his jeans and kicked off his shoes. "You pitch or catch?"

"Switch."

The twink sniggered. "So you catch but you don't want to admit it."

"Little boy, I could bend you over the shelves and fuck you dizzy," Ken retorted.

The twink shoved down his jeans and kicked them off. "Take your best shot, Dad."

Dan gestured at one of the onlookers. The man paled and pointed at himself.

"Towel," Dan said.

"Oh, oh right," the man said, laughing nervously. "Where's my head at." He handed over the clean, red towel hanging over his shoulder. He flushed as Dan gave him a brief, almost cursory glance.

Dan threw the towel to Chad. "Wipe off the bench."

Chad licked his lips and threw himself into the task, scrubbing every inch of the bench with his towel.

"Hey!" the last user of the bench protested, "I'm not that—" He trailed off at Dan's look.

Chad fastidiously folded the towel and handed it back to its owner. He'd watched with jealousy and a growing sense of arousal as Andrew had knelt like a supplicant. Now he was oppressively aware of the other men around him as he pushed down his sweatpants. He was aware of Andrew, watching and smirking.

He heard Dan stroll over and felt Dan's finger walk along his forearm. Chad turned and saw something like a smile or a snarl touch the corner of Dan's mouth. With Dan it was difficult to be certain, perhaps there was no difference. Dan captured Chad's gaze until Chad looked away.

"You might say please," Chad managed.

Dan chuckled, a low, throaty laugh. "You might. Many have."

Chad licked his lips. "Please?"

Dan nodded at the bench. Chad could feel him watching as he took a deep breath and then bent down, bracing his hands on the bench. Chad felt his ankles being nudged wider apart with Dan's foot. Then Dan's hand was on Chad's ass, pinching the firm skin between his thumb and forefinger. Chad licked his lips, wondering would come next. He heard a slight intake from the men around them and felt Dan's hand lightly slap his buttock. It was a sting, and then he felt the burst of warmth as blood rushed to the area.

"Hey!" Andrew protested weakly.

"Shut up," Chad muttered as Dan slapped him again.

"Be a good boy or you don't get to watch," Dan said.

Chad heard the rustle and thump of Dan pushing down his pants and boxers to the floor. He shivered when he heard Dan snap his fingers at the general assembly.

"Condom," Dan said.

A score of foil wrapped little packets rained at Chad's feet. He heard Dan whistle lightly as he ducked down to pick one up. Chad jumped as Dan flicked Chad's ass with a finger. Chad raised his head as he heard Dan opening the condom wrapper. Andrew was watching with a mixture of shock and arousal. Chad smiled at his lover and then dropped his gaze.

Dan rested his right hand on Chad's ass as he reached around to stroke the other man's cock. Chad shifted his weight slightly; Dan was leaning against him and he could feel his tendons and ligaments stretching. It wasn't uncomfortable, yet. He almost jumped as Dan grasped his cock in a strong, commanding grip. He grew quickly to hardness as Dan pumped him with swift and brutal expertise. Chad's head hung down and of his audience all he could see were their feet, but he could hear their breathing and muttered comments.

He felt Dan's hand grip his hip and then Dan's cock thrust inside him. Chad moaned and felt himself rock forward onto his palms. He felt himself pushed up onto his tiptoes as Dan's thrusts came hard and deep. Chad groaned as he felt Dan's balls slap heavily against his ass, felt Dan's hand bruising his hip and felt the heat of Dan's breath on the back of his neck.

Chad squeezed his eyes shut. Heat was pooling in his groin and his awareness of the world was shrinking to his panting breath and hammering heart. Chad's fingers clawed at the bench and light burst across his closed eyes. He came with a creaking moan, spurting streams onto the floor, the bench and his own shoes. There were sniggers and catcalls from the audience but Chad didn't hear them. He knew nothing until he gradually became aware of his body moving, of his arms and legs shaking slightly as Dan continued to fuck him. He realized that Dan was holding him in place with an arm around his waist. That arm tightened as Dan came. Chad gripped the bench as Dan's weight pressed heavily against him, and then was gone. Chad yelped as Dan slapped his ass.

"Don't take all day," Dan said.

Chad gingerly turned around and collapsed down onto the bench as Dan pulled up his pants and strolled away.

The twink wrapped his legs around Ken's waist as he was lifted up and crushed against the wall. He bit at Ken's mouth as his fingers grabbed at Ken's hair. Ken's fingers sank into his thighs as he supported the twink's weight.

"Come on," the twink moaned.

"Patience, little boy," Ken muttered. He shifted position, feeling his arms complain and ignoring it, and then thrust quickly.

The twink threw back his head, banging it against the wall, and tightened his grip around Ken's waist. His fingers twisted in Ken's hair, pulling his face closer, as they panted into each other's mouths.

"Harder," the twink demanded.

"Shut up."

The twink laughed and gave Ken a hard kiss. "You wanna pretend I'm your boy, the one on the bars? Fuck that. Look me in the face when you fuck me."

"You're nothing like him," Ken gasped.

"I'm better than him." The twink dropped his hands and raked his nails along Ken's shoulders. "He won't fuck you."

"You talk too much." Ken dropped his weight forward as he came, crushing the twink between his body and the wall.

"Next time you'll have to gag me," the twink said, pushing his hair out of his eyes. He slid his hand between their bodies to take himself in hand.

"Don't tempt me," Ken grumbled.

"Maybe tie me up too," the twink said, closing his eyes.

"Blindfold?" Ken suggested, lifting his head.

"Helpless."

Ken pressed his lips to the twink's ear. "I could tie you to the balance bar. Blindfolded and gagged. Not knowing who was touching you, licking you, fucking you."

The twink's feet drummed against Ken's ass as he came, groaning deep in the back of his throat. He dropped his forehead against Ken's shoulder and let out a heavy sigh.

"Great."

"Great for you, I think my arms are about to drop off," Ken muttered.

Angel hurried along the corridor. He didn't know where Ken had gone and frankly he didn't much care. What was playing on his mind was finding the weight room before Ken found him. He didn't know if there was any fun to be had there but he was damn sure there was no fun to be had with Ken.

As he loped along the cool corridor he attracted plenty of attention, but he had his sights set on a bigger prey. He slipped into the weight room and found the smell of sex and the mild embarrassment of near strangers pushed into intimacy. There were a mix of ages but most of them seemed either tense or sheepish. None of them had the swaggering confidence Angel expected to see from the man he was seeking.

"You lost, lad?" asked one of the men.

"Someone told me Dan Lyon might be in here," Angel said blithely.

Two of the men at a bench, a couple in matching sweats, exchanged knowing glances.

"You missed him, kid," the short, stocky one said.

"He's gone to the locker room," said the other one.

"Thanks very much," Angel said nicely, turning to stroll away.

He ignored the bickering that broke out behind him. The locker room wasn't far away and anticipation put a zest in his step. Ken wouldn't approve, but Ken didn't approve of much. Angel suspected that the other man was nervous the infamous Dan Lyon wouldn't *want* to screw him.

Angel pushed open the door to the locker room and sauntered in. The room had the same scent of socks, sweat and Axe body spray as locker rooms everywhere. It was empty apart from the leonine man dressing in the corner. He was a little shorter than Angel, but broad and muscular. His thick, fair hair fell to his shoulders in loose curls and there was a stylized tattoo of a roaring lion on his back. Angel let the door swing shut behind him and watched as the other man cocked his head.

"You lost, little boy?"

Angel stepped forward, and realized that the man was standing in front of a speckled and scratched mirror.

"I'm exactly where I was planning to be."

The man turned. He was handsome in a hard, self-aware way and he looked Angel over with frank appraisal. Although he was only a few years older than Angel he obviously meant himself to be intimidating. He sauntered over to Angel and raised an eyebrow when Angel stood his ground.

"I don't know you."

"I don't know you either."

"I'm Dan Lyon," he said. It was said calmly, not a boast but he was expecting the name to be recognized, and the meaning to be understood.

"My trainer makes sure we're not here when you are," Angel said. "But today couldn't be helped." He shrugged easily.

"He doesn't want you around me."

"Or he doesn't want you around him, I'm not sure." Angel smiled sweetly. "You're not a particular topic of conversation."

Lyon chuckled and shook his head. "He's not here. You are. Why's that?"

"Reasons," Angel said, smiling.

Ken stomped along the cold corridor, his soles squeaking on the hard floor. When he'd returned to the floor there had been no sign of Angel. He'd checked all the little rooms in which Angel could have secreted himself and found nothing. Asking around had got very little information until he reached the weight room where the answers he got had not pleased him.

He grabbed the door to the locker room and yanked it open. He paused before he stepped into the room, listening to the sound of the showers. Ken swore softly and stepped into the locker room, shutting the door behind him. Someone had left open the door between the showers and the locker room, allowing steam to swirl around the locker room and condense onto the cold metal doors. Ken heard a moan from the beyond. He cautiously opened the door and peered into the steamy, humid room.

He saw two young men, naked and soaking wet. The taller had long blond hair pushed back from his face and a lion tattoo on his back. Water poured down his skin, flowed around his muscles and pooled around his feet. The other...the other was Angel. His dark hair was slicked down against his skull and streams of water flowed down his treasure trail and into his groin. The blond and Angel were wrestling for dominance; pushing, shoving, slipping and sliding as they groped, grabbed, kissed, bit, scratched and thrust.

Ken leaned against the door frame. Lyon and Angel were oblivious to his presence. He watched Angel snigger as he pushed Lyon against the wall, and nip as his throat. Angel's body was slim and toned. Lyon's hands passed over it hungrily, caressing his thighs, ass and back. How many other men had those hands possessed and how many hands would enjoy Angel? Ken slid his hand into his sweats and wrapped it around his cock. It swelled at his touch, excited at the sight and sounds in front of him.

Lyon's hands gripped Angel's ass and pulled him closer, his fingers massaging the creamy, fine flesh. He lowered his face to bite Angel's shoulder, wide, deep, sucking bites that made Angel grunt and rake his nails down Lyon's back. Angel's fingertips caressed the mane of the lion tattoo and ran with the steaming water. Lyon gripped Angel's thighs and lifted him slightly, bringing the younger man up to his tiptoes. Lyon thrust between Angel's thighs, his cock sandwiched between the strong, taut legs. He came with a deep growl that made Ken's breathing deepen.

As Lyon closed his eyes and breathed deeply, Angel stepped back. He wrapped his hand around his cock and used long, deliberate strokes to urge it to completion. He rested his other hand against the wall as he leaned forward. His shoulders shook as his ejaculate pumped out, spattering against Lyon's stomach and groin. Lyon's eyes snapped open and stared at Angel in stunned surprise. Angel laughed, and kissed him once. Then turned and sauntered toward the door.

"Enjoying the view?"

"I don't... I just..."

"I wouldn't let him catch you there," Angel said, "he'd eat you alive."

# BAGGED

## Jake Rich

When a couple of the trainers at the boxing gym mentioned hanging out after closing time one Friday night, I thought for sure I'd finally died and gone to heaven. I can't ever get enough of that place. In fact the L Street Ring is just about the only place you'll find me these days, except for doing the nine to five thing. Hell, I get high just walking in there.

It's the sounds that always hit me first. The timer, buzzing out a three-minute round, a thirty-second warning and a one-minute rest. The grunts from throwing punch combos on the heavy bags. The three-beat rhythm of speed bags and the sound of air being sliced to bits with jump ropes. And that's nothing compared to what you see.

First thing I saw was a heavy bag swinging on a chain from the ceiling. Then one of the trainers grabbed it with a bear hug and held it so another obvious newbie could try out the one-two combination.

"Keep your chin in, your elbows in. One. Two. See? That's better. One, two, one, two. That's it. Keep moving around the bag." The trainer let go of the bag and gave it a little push so it had some sway to it. Then he saw me trying to figure out what the hell I was even doing there. I was just standing there looking lost and watching sweat, fists and feet flying all over the place.

Then some blood splattered to the floor from a busted-up nose.

"Who'd you be?" the trainer asked, walking over to me.

"Phil. I'm new here."

"Yeah, you're new to here all right. You got Mexican wraps and gloves? Get changed, then come get me. I'll wrap your hands for you."

"Cool," I managed to say. "Thanks."

My head was already speeding like a freight train as I changed from jeans and boots to sweats and sneaks. Fuck, this guy's biceps were bigger than my head. How the hell did he get arms like that? I'd bet his cock was just as thick. Damn. He hadn't even said his name. *Fuck me hard, please, Sir. And by the way what's your name, Sir?* ran through my brain and down to my dick.

My nerves were live wires as I looked around for the hunk with no name. He was in the ring, working mitts with a young kid, couldn't have been more than ten years old. The round had just started, so I stood near the ropes and watched. I didn't really know what was going on, and I didn't really care. I just wanted to watch this hot guy move around the ring.

He was easy on the kid but worked him hard enough to sweat some. The buzzer warned thirty seconds to go, and the kid barely made it to the one-minute rest. They touched mitt to glove, stepped between the ropes and out of the ring.

"Hey, Phil, got your wraps?"

I nodded and followed him over to a corner that was quiet, compared to the rest of the place.

"Okay. First thing is to unroll and find the thumb hook."

"Why is it so long?" I asked, surprised by how much it unwound.

"Because you're going to need all the knuckle protection you can get. Now grab it and wrap it around and over the back of your hand like this."

Already I was confused and frustrated. Wrap this here, and then around there, and through that and back around here again. And do the same thing only opposite for your other hand. Dude, you gotta be kiddin' me.

"Can you slow down there ah...what's your name again?"

"Jackson. Jackson's my name."

"Glad to meet you, Jackson. So how'd you get biceps like that?" I asked as I unwrapped and rewrapped my right hand three times.

"Fried chicken."

"What? No, seriously. How'd you get your arms so big? I've always wanted huge biceps, but I can't ever make it happen."

"Fried chicken," he said again, and laughed.

Yeah, that's Jackson for you, always joking. But only half joking, 'cause when he's not training for a fight, he's sitting on the edge of the ring knocking back Mickey Dee's burgers and fries for lunch. Every day.

I'm happy for the invite, especially since I don't know the guys as much as I'd like to. It's only been six months since I joined. Six months, and I still don't have a clue how to throw a half-ass jab, much less a decent one.

I am getting better on the speed bag though. My first time on it I hit it so hard I popped the thing. That's how I got the name Freak tagged on me. They took a liking to me right then and there. They rank on you all the time, if they like you. I kinda figured that I'd be one of the boys eventually, especially with Jackson yelling out "Freak" whenever I walk in the place, and the whole time I'm there too. He's yelling out "Freak" and then laughing, making sure everybody hears him above the noise and hip-hop tunes.

I haven't even mentioned TJ yet. He's the other trainer that gets me hard. Totally the opposite of Jackson. More on the quiet side, he doesn't like loads of attention. For some reason, just about everything anybody says to him makes him blush. I'm always real careful about not getting caught looking at his package. Not sure if he'd just blush or punch me out. Probably both. Hard as I try not to, I end up staring right at it, looking and drooling and hoping that someday soon he'll take me up the ass.

He's always asking me what I'm doing over the weekend. He's single and a little lonely, like me. His fiancée broke up with him after he had another run in with the law.

Both he and Jackson have that in common—spending more than a night or two in the jailhouse. Jackson did a couple of years for a drug deal. TJ doesn't ever say what he was in for, and I figure it makes sense not to be asking him about it.

"What are you up to, Phil?" TJ comes walking over to me during a minute rest. "Anything good going on?"

"Yeah, I'm going to a party tomorrow night," I say.

"A birthday party?"

"Nope, this is no birthday party. It's a different kind of party. Maybe you'd be interested in going…ah, well…maybe…not." Holy fuck, what the hell am I doing inviting him to Leather Night? Am I crazy?

"Knowing you, Phil, it's got to be something freaky," TJ says.

The buzzer goes off, and I laugh as the place explodes with noise again. I get into stance for my next punch, then cock my head toward him.

"It takes one to know one TJ." I smirk, then throw three right hooks in a row. His face turns red and he walks off toward the ring. I know he's gonna be after me to do mitts with him now.

He finishes three rounds with a middle-aged guy, who's probably just a couple years younger than me and in better shape. Then he comes looking for me, and I'm doing my best to hide behind one of the heavy bags.

"Phil!" TJ yells in my direction. "Let's go, you're up next."

Damn it, why didn't I leave before now? I already did three rounds on the speed bag, five rounds on the heavy bag, plus abs, leg work and some shadowboxing. I'm beat and ready to head home.

"Nah, thanks but no thanks, TJ. I'm done for the day."

I prefer doing mitts with him, instead of Jackson. TJ will work with you. He knows just how far he can push you, and takes you just past that. Jackson flat-out pushes you over a cliff and laughs the whole time he's doing it.

"Phil! Let's go!"

Fuck. Ring time for me is like being worked over with a cat-o'-nine-tails. I fucking hate it while it's happening, but damn, it sure feels good when it's over.

"All right, all right already, give me a second here." I walk over to the ring, hop up and awkwardly slide through the ropes. I run my gloved hand across my forehead and wipe away sweat that's headed straight for my eyes.

"Ready? Remember, put your whole body into it. Don't just punch out from your waist, follow it through with your shoulder, back and legs. Okay?"

I shake my head yes, and place my hands and feet. TJ always starts out with a straight jab, which is the hardest throw for me. Then he calls out punch combos: one-two-five, two-four-two, three-four-one. And just like always, I get pissed off 'cause I don't know which hand to throw and when. Why can't I remember that one is a straight left, two is a right hook and three is a left hook? TJ tells me to calm down, then slows the pace enough so I can think about what I'm doing. I'm finally getting my combos worked out when the warning buzzer goes off. Fuck. I know for sure what combo TJ wants next. Really fast four-fives. Do you have an idea how long thirty seconds is, throwing nothing but four-fives?

"Go another round?" TJ asks as the one-minute rest starts.

"Yeah, sure," I say, breathing heavy.

Little over two minutes into the next round, I'm toast. Got rubber for arms, and I can't catch my breath. I stop, then double over, trying to force air down my lungs.

"You're not breathing right," TJ says. "Throw your punch breathing out, then right away breathe *in*, not out again. You're holding your breath. Come on, let's go. You got thirty seconds left on the clock."

I'm not moving. I'm just sucking down air.

"Phil, don't make me do mouth to mouth on you."

Still bent over, I turn my head and look up at him.

"Yeah, you wish," I say, raising my eyebrows and laughing between gulps of air. There's just no way I can do another round, and TJ doesn't even ask. He does throw some encouraging words my way, which I thank him for, and we touch mitt to glove. I push on the rope and bend down. I swing my leg over the rope, trying to climb out of the ring. TJ opens the ropes wider for me, and I'm moving through when I plant face-first into TJ's crotch. It happens so fast, and is over so fast, I think maybe I just imagined it. It did happen though, 'cause just then he'd moved in close enough for me get a good eyeful, and a good whiff too. I sucked in his sweaty balls smell; it was just one gulp of air, but it was enough to get to me.

He doesn't say anything, and I don't either. I head off to change, wondering what's going on with TJ. Maybe I really will get pounded by him. I'm getting hard, and taking off my sweats doesn't help any. I can't stop from giving my cock a couple of good spanks, then hurry up getting dressed. I already know I'm jerking off as soon as I get home.

I usually say goodbye before I leave, so I walk out of the changing room to find TJ and Jackson. They're hanging out right around the corner, and I just about crash into them.

"We're thinking of closing early tonight. John's not here, so he won't know anything different anyway," TJ says. "Give us half an hour tops and we'll head over to the Happy Swallow for a couple of beers."

"Ah...sure, why not, I guess can hang out for a couple of hours tonight. I'll wait for you guys up front."

Holy fuck. First a face full of TJ, then a beer invite. Today sure went from shitty to awesome real fast. I've been here before when they closed early because the owner had gone home. But I've never been asked to stick around afterward.

I'm ducking and punching my reflection in the front-desk window, trying to steady my nerves. TJ is laughing in the back while Jackson is yelling about something, then TJ stops laughing and yells back at Jackson. I can't hear what all the hollering is about, but it sounds bad. I'm thinking what the fuck, I'm sitting here waiting for these two and they start a fight. Should I just leave or go back there? And do what? Break up a fight between a pro and semipro boxer? Yeah, right.

The shouting is still going on, so I decide to head home. I shove the crash bar and bang my head on the damn door. It's not opening. I shove it harder thinking it's just stuck, and still nothing. Are you shittin' me, man? I'm locked inside the gym. Great. I rattle the door some, expecting nothing and getting it. Now what? Only thing I can do is find TJ and Jackson.

I walk back to the ring room. Most of the lights are off, and everything's kind of spooky. The yelling isn't as loud now; I'm hoping they've calmed down enough that we can finally go for that beer.

"Hey guys, what's up? Can we go get a beer now? Or at least unlock the door so I can get out of here?"

"You ain't going nowhere, Freak." I'm hearing Jackson, but I'm not seeing him in the low light.

"Hey, Jackson! What the fuck is going on, man? Why you two yelling?"

"We're not yelling, we're just having loud conversation... about you, Freakazoid."

"What about me?"

"Well see, Jackson wants to do you first," TJ says. "And I think I should do you first."

"Do...do...what...first?" I'm trying not to stammer while I damn near shit my pants and get a hard-on all at the same time.

"Oh yeah, like you don't know what TJ means," Jackson says. "TJ, let's show the Freak here what you yelling about."

The lights come on; a hand grabs me by the back of my neck, and shoves me to the floor. "So Freak, how many push-ups can you really do?" TJ asks.

I scramble into position and start pumping them out fast. Jackson's got his foot hovering above my ass and pushes me down whenever I break form. I don't know how many I'm doing, but my arms are shaking real bad and I'm thinking they're going to give out soon.

"Working hard are ya, Phil? It's about time you did," Jackson says, pushing me to the floor and keeping me there with his foot. I'm crumpled up in a heap, my arms still quivering. I tell myself to just go with this; don't think about it, just go along for the ride.

"Don't you think so, Freak?" Jackson says, real loud this time.

"You think we don't see you hiding in the bag corner, but we do," Jackson says.

"I see you all the time hiding back there."

"Now get up!" Jackson grabs the back of my belt and pulls me up to my feet. He's still got a good hold on me when he reaches around the front and unbuckles my belt. TJ steps in and pulls my jeans and boxers down to my knees. Then they both have a good laugh 'cause it's as plain as day that I'm enjoying all this.

"Will ya look at that...what you got going on here, Mr. Freaky Deaky?" Jackson says, laughing.

I feel heat in my face, and I know I'm blushing. TJ laughs and his face turns beet red too. Maybe it's my imagination, but his sweats seem to be bulging out more than usual.

"It's time we see just how much you got, Freak." Jackson tugs at my T-shirt. I lift my arms up and he pulls my shirt off. "TJ, help him out of his pants there." I'm pushed down to the floor, and TJ pulls off my boots and my jeans. Now I got a boner, and I'm naked too. All I can think is that I hope they plow my ass good. I want it so bad it hurts.

TJ picks up a pair of wraps, and roughly tapes up my hands. Keeping his eyes locked on mine, he pulls me up into the ring, where Jackson is waiting.

"You're bragging about fighting at Golden Gloves next year. By then you might get lucky and not get killed in the first round," Jackson says. "You're lazy. You're out of shape. You have no discipline. You can work a lot harder than you do, and starting right now that's what you're gonna do."

I'm in the center of the ring, following orders; round after round of jumping jacks, crunches, running in place, side-step running, medicine ball work. Over to the speed bag, back into the ring. Two rounds of foot work, then over to the double-end bag for three rounds. I'm worn out, I'm crashing and my dick is going soft.

"Please guys. Can we stop now? Please?"

"You stop when we say you stop," Jackson says. "Next three rounds you're doing inchworm."

I fucking hate doing the inchworm. But sticking my ass in the air in front of TJ and Jackson is hot as hell. When I bend over, Jackson takes a swipe at my ass with a doubled-up jump rope. The sting brings up more heat, and beads of sweat drop to the floor. My dick gets hard again.

"Hey TJ! Look what Freak's up to," Jackson says. "You really like getting your ass beat, don't you, Freak? Bend over and grab your ankles, boy."

Again, I do what I'm told. I close my eyes, hold my breath and wait. And wait some more. Fuck, what the shit is going on? Will somebody please pound my ass, already! I hear some noise, so I open my eyes. I watch TJ give Jackson a blow job upside down. I can hardly keep from grabbing my dick and jerking off. I'm whimpering to myself. Or at least I thought I was.

"What's the matter, Freak Man, you got blue balls?" Jackson says, pulling out of TJ's mouth. "You want my junk, Freak Man?"

"He's been checking out my junk since his first day here," TJ says.

"Is that right?" Jackson says, laughing. "If you want it that bad, then worm your ass over here."

I drop to the floor, embarrassed that TJ knows I've been staring at his package all this time. I work my way over, ending up on my stomach at Jackson's feet.

"Pick him up, TJ, and sling him over the ropes."

TJ picks me up and damn near throws me over his shoulder, then puts me inside the ring. He brings me to a corner, bends me over and tells me to wrap my arms around the corner cushion. I do as he says. My arms and legs are shaking. I think it's mostly because I'm excited; that and muscle fatigue too. I concentrate on stopping, or at least slowing down my jitters. I lean my head into the cushion, and that gives me some relief.

I hear TJ spit into his hands, just as the three-minute buzzer goes off. Without a word, he finds my hole, and pushes his cock through. Something close to a scream comes out of me, and it won't stop.

"Fuck! Why you screaming like that? Shut the fuck up or I'll fucking shut you up!" Jackson yells.

I bite down hard on my lip. TJ bangs me so fucking hard my head crashes into the cushion every second or so. He keeps pumping for the whole round. He pulls out for the one-minute rest, and I see Jackson out of the corner of my eye. Jackson jumps into the ring, doing his usual footwork waiting for the next round to start.

"Get ready, Freak, 'cause here I come." He spits on my hole, then pulls me open and spits inside. He slides right in and laughs as he pounds me hard. I taste blood as my teeth cut through my lip. I hold on with one hand, grab my cock with the other and yank off, spraying the cushion and my arm.

"Figures you couldn't last two rounds, Freak," Jackson says. "I got at least two more rounds left in me. How many more you got, TJ?"

"You're not beating me out, Jackson. If you got two more rounds to go, then I got three."

I lick the blood from my lip and get ready to go the distance.

# ABOUT THE
# AUTHORS

**BRENT ARCHER** (brentarcher.net) has had stories published with Cleis Press, House of Erotica and most recently his first novel *The Bastard's Key*, as well as two short stories, "Halfway out of the Dark," and "The Christmas Proposal," with MuseItHOT Publishing. When not writing, Brent's other job is in a theater.

**MICHAEL BRACKEN** is the author of several books and more than one thousand short stories, including erotic fiction published in *Best Gay Erotica 2013*, *Best Gay Romance 2010* and *2013*, *Model Men*, *Pledges*, *Ultimate Gay Erotica 2006* and many other anthologies and magazines. He lives and writes in Texas.

**R. W. CLINGER** (rwclinger.com) is the author of *Cutie Pie Must Die*, *The Pool Boy*, *Nebraska Close*, *Beneath the Boarder*, *Bearology 101*, *Skin Tour* and *Skin Artist*. His series, the Stockton County Cowboys, includes *Chasing Cowboys*, *Riding Cowboys*, *Roping Cowboys* and *Branding Cowboys*.

**LANDON DIXON**'s writing credits include stories in the anthologies *I Like It Like That, Brief Encounters, Hot Daddies, Unzipped, Wild Boys, Bad Boys, Straight No More, Team Players, Homo Thugs, Nasty Boys, Ultimate Gay Erotica*, and *Best Gay Erotica*, and his own *Hot Tales of Gay Lust 1, 2* and *3*.

**KATYA HARRIS** (misskatyaharris.wordpress.com) has been published by Dreamspinner Press (*A Life Without*), and has had stories included in several anthologies such as *Boys In Bed* (Xcite Books), *Blood Embrace* and *Dark Menagerie* (Storm Moon Press). She lives and works in the United Kingdom.

**FOX LEE** (sinauthor@gmail.com) is a writer published in several anthologies, including *Nasty Boys* (Cleis Press) and *Lover Boys Forever* (Starbooks Press). Married to a man from Hong Kong, Fox is well aware of the virile beauty and splendor of Asian males.

**JEFF MANN** has published three poetry chapbooks, three full-length books of poetry, two collections of personal essays, a volume of memoir and poetry, two novellas, two novels and two collections of short fiction. He teaches creative writing at Virginia Tech in Blacksburg, Virginia.

**GREGORY L. NORRIS** has written for television and numerous national magazines. Norris judged for the 2012 Lambda Awards, and is the author of the flash fiction collection, *Shrunken Heads: Twenty Tiny Tales of Mystery and Terror*. He writes from the outer limits of New Hampshire.

**SASHA PAYNE** is an English writer of gay erotic fiction and romance. She is a lifelong speculative fiction and fantasy fan and most enjoys working within the genres of speculative fiction, fantasy or historical fiction.

**OLEANDER PLUME** (poisonpendirtymind.com) writes erotica in several genres. Her work can be found in *The Women Who Love to Love Gay Romance,* edited by Ryan Field, *Best Women's Erotica 2014,* edited by Violet Blue and *Take This Man,* edited by Neil Plakcy.

**JAKE RICH** lives in the Greater Boston area, where he owns a home inhabited by mice. His work appears in *Rode Hard, Put Away Wet,* from Suspect Thoughts Press, *Hard Road, Easy Riding,* from Haworth Press, and *Ultimate Gay Erotica 2009,* from Alyson Books.

**ROB ROSEN** (therobrosen.com), author of the novels *Sparkle:The Queerest Book You'll Ever Love, Divas Las Vegas, Hot Lava, Southern Fried, Queerwolf, Vamp, Queens of the Apocalypse, Creature Comfort* and *Fate,* has had short stories featured in more than two hundred anthologies.

Residing on English Bay in Vancouver, Canada, **JAY STARRE** has pumped out steamy gay fiction for dozens of anthologies and has written two gay erotic novels.

**BOB VICKERY**'s stories have been published in four written collections (*Skin Deep, Cock Tales, Cocksure* and *Play Buddies*) and two audio books (*Man Jack* and *Hunting For Sailors*). He currently resides in San Francisco.

**LOGAN ZACHARY** (loganzacharydicklit.com) lives in Minneapolis, MN and has over a hundred erotic stories in print. *Calendar Boys* is a collection of his short stories. *Big Bad Wolf* is an erotic werewolf mystery set in Northern Minnesota and its sequel *GingerDead Man* will be out later this year.

# ABOUT
# THE EDITOR

**SHANE ALLISON'S** editing career began with the bestselling gay erotic anthology *Hot Cops: Gay Erotic Stories*, which was one of his proudest moments. Since the birth of his first anthology, he has gone on to publish over a dozen gay erotica anthologies such as *Straight Guys: Gay Erotic Fantasies, Cruising: Gay Erotic Stories, Middle Men: Gay Erotic Three-somes, Frat Boys: Gay Erotic Stories, Brief Encounters: 69 Hot Gay Shorts, College Boys: Gay Erotic Stories, Hardworking Men: Gay Erotic Fiction, Hot Cops: Gay Erotic Fiction, Back-draft: Fireman Erotica* and *Afternoon Pleasures: Erotica for Gay Couples*. Shane Allison has appeared in five editions *of Best Gay Erotica, Best Black Gay Erotica* and *Zane's Z-Rated: Chocolate Flava 3*. His debut poetry collection, *Slut Machine* is out from Queer Mojo and his poem/memoir *I Remember* is out from Future Tense Books. Shane is at work on his second novel and currently resides in Tallahassee, Florida.

Printed in the United States
By Bookmasters